Hunter Squadron
Yeoman in the Congo Conflict

Robert Jackson

© Robert Jackson 1984

Robert Jackson has asserted his rights under the Copyright, Design and Patents Act, 1988, to be identified as the author of this work.

First published in 1984 by George Weidenfeld and Nicholson Ltd.

This edition published in 2016 by Endeavour Press Ltd.

Chapter One

SEEN FROM A HEIGHT OF FORTY-FIVE THOUSAND FEET, THE island of Helgoland was a featureless grey blob, set in a sea that mirrored the sunlight like dark-green glass, its fringes marked by a thin white line of surf.

It was a morning to remember; a glorious morning of high summer, unmasked by even a hint of cloud. Only in the south, where the sun stood high in a white glare, was the horizon hard to distinguish; elsewhere its curve was crisp and sharp, broken in the north-east by the long scatter of the North Frisian Islands.

Towards the islands sixteen aircraft flew, cleaving through the stratosphere, their condensation trails etched stark and white against the green backcloth of the sea eight miles below. They were Hawker Hunter Mk6 jet fighters, graceful swept-wing descendants of the famous Hurricanes that had fought so valiantly to sweep Hitler's Luftwaffe from the skies of England twenty years earlier.

The squadron of Hunters that flew high over the North Sea on this summer's day in 1960 was normally based at Rheinbrücken, near Hamborn in northern Germany, which it shared with two other Hunter units. For the past few days, however, the sixteen fighters had been deployed to the island of Sylt, which lay off the coast of Schleswig-Holstein close to the Danish border; this was the location of the RAF 2nd Tactical Air Force's Weapons Training Unit, where fighter squadrons in Germany were periodically sent to carry out air-to-air and air-to-ground firing practice.

The Hunters were flying in squadron battle formation, the aircraft in each section positioned in the classic 'finger four' grouping first perfected by the Luftwaffe and since used by air forces all over the world. First, and lowest of the formation, came the four Hunters of Red Section, with Yellow Section on their left and a little higher up. Astern of these two sections, and higher still, were the aircraft of Blue Section, and on their left, the topmost element of the formation, was Green Section.

The sun was on the right of the formation and astern, in the four o'clock position. In its glare, several thousand feet higher than the others, a seventeenth aircraft flew. They knew it was there, for although it was almost invisible against the intense light its long contrail betrayed its presence.

In the cockpit of the seventeenth Hunter, Group Captain George Yeoman hummed contentedly to himself behind his oxygen mask, one gloved hand resting lightly on the control column, the other on his left thigh. This, he thought, more than compensated for the long desk-bound hours demanded of him by his post of Officer Commanding, RAF Rheinbrücken; the sad thing was that such opportunities to escape into what he considered to be his natural element were becoming less frequent as time went by.

At the age of forty, after a flying career with the Royal Air Force spanning more than twenty years, George Yeoman knew that retirement was creeping over the horizon. He would see out his quarter-century, maybe, and leave at forty-five; he knew that he could go on for ten more years after that, and gain further promotion, but somehow there didn't seem to be much point. He had no wish to end his career in stagnation behind a Ministry desk after an active operational life that had started in the Battle of France, in May 1940.

There was another tour ahead of him; maybe he would opt for a liaison job in the United States to round things off. There were some plum exchange postings for senior RAF officers with the USAF, and a couple of years with Air Defense Command HQ in Colorado would be right up his street. Maybe his old pal General Jim Callender, who had once served alongside Yeoman in the early days of the Second World War, could pull a few strings in that direction.

A tour in the USA would certainly please Yeoman's American-born wife, Julia. It was a long time since she had been back home. Also, a couple of years in America would be a good education for their two children, eleven-year-old June and little Paul, who was six.

That was in the future. In the meantime, Yeoman, with no clear idea about what he intended to do when he left the RAF, meant to make the most of any flying that came his way.

This morning's exercise was more in the nature of a joyride than anything else. He did not need to be there, shadowing the Hunter formation, but he was interested to see how the pilots would perform in a few minutes' time against the 'opposition' which, unknown to them, was even now racing towards them from the direction of the Danish coast, just below contrail level.

The opposition, he knew, would be making a fast climbing attack on the Hunters from the seven o'clock position. He knew exactly where to look, and after a while his vigil was rewarded by the sight of six metallic arrows, coming up hard from the north-west after flying a long curve out over the sea. The 'enemy' could afford to attack on the climb, for their speed was a good deal higher than the Hunters'. They were North American F-100 Super Sabres of the US 3rd Air Force, temporarily deployed to Denmark from their normal base at Wethersfield, in the United Kingdom, and they were capable of a top speed of 900 mph at forty thousand feet, a good 200 mph more than the British fighters.

Speed, however, was fine when it came to overhauling one's target or getting out of a tight spot, but Yeoman knew from long experience that the outcome of an air battle was usually decided by superior manoeuvrability. In this respect, the Hunter could outclass the F-100 every time.

Contrails had begun to form behind the Super Sabres now, and the Hunter pilots had spotted them. Yeoman watched with interest and a good deal of professional pride as the Hunters, section by section and still holding formation, executed an immaculate defensive break, turning hard to meet the threat and presenting the American pilots with a maximum deflection shot. They would not have much to show on their camera-gun films for this first firing pass.

Far from manoeuvrable at high speed, the F-100s passed through the middle of the Hunter formation, whose sections had turned left and right, and went up to fifty thousand feet with afterburners blazing. They made a broad turn, splitting into two elements of three as they did so, and came down hard to attack on the dive.

As Yeoman watched intently, losing height gradually to keep pace with the descending battle, he saw the silver dart shapes of four more F-100s arrowing down from the north, on a level with the Hunters. While twelve of the latter carried on turning to confront the diving Super Sabres, the remaining four broke hard left to meet the new batch of Americans head-on.

Yeoman saw a definite pattern starting to emerge from the mock combat, and nodded in approval. The leader of the Hunter squadron, while parrying each new thrust made by the American fighters, was losing height continuously, his object being to get the F-100s down to sea level where they would be forced into a turning fight. After each pass by the American fighters, sections of Hunters were diving steeply away, pulling up only briefly to meet fresh attacks.

The mêlée dropped through twenty thousand feet and went on descending. Yeoman went down with it, keeping his distance, casting an eye from time to time on the Hunter's fuel gauges; in another few minutes, it would be time to go home.

A silvery flash off to the right caught his attention and he turned his head in that direction, scanning the sky. About a mile away, a lone F-100 was turning towards him, closing rapidly. Yeoman grinned in delight; he had been expecting something of the sort. One of the Yanks was trying to 'zap' him, to use their jargon.

He rolled the Hunter on to its back and pulled through on the stick, taking the fighter seawards in a vertical dive. The whisper of the airflow outside the cockpit became harsh as the speed built up. On the instrument panel, the needle of the Machmeter trembled through 0.95 and went on rising slowly towards 1.0, the speed of sound.

The Super Sabre continued to follow him, still narrowing the distance. Yeoman eased back the control column gently until the Hunter was speeding straight and level, a few hundred feet above the sea. Misty pressure waves danced back over its wings. The speed started to fall away as Yeoman continued his level run; a check rearwards showed that the F-100 was still with him, almost within firing distance.

Slender contrails streamed from the Hunter's wingtips as Yeoman broke to port in a maximum-rate turn, his vision blurring as the high 'g' forced him down in his ejection seat. The F-100 pilot tried to follow suit, as Yeoman had anticipated, and failed to match the British fighter's manoeuvrability. The heavy Super Sabre skidded across the sky, carried on by its momentum, and Yeoman hoped that the American pilot was experienced; only a couple of weeks earlier, an F-100 had tried to better a Hunter in a low-level turning combat off the Suffolk coast and had flicked into the sea.

This American, Yeoman soon discovered, was not going to risk his neck. Climbing away, he made a couple of diving passes at the Hunter, which Yeoman avoided by steep-turning, and then reduced speed and came alongside, rocking his wings to show that as far as he was concerned, the contest was over. Yeoman stuck two fingers up at him, grinning behind his face mask; the American reciprocated and then accelerated away, his turbojet leaving a thick trail of dark fuel smoke as he climbed towards the Danish coast.

Yeoman gained altitude too, although in more leisurely fashion, and set course for Sylt. Over the radio, he heard the leader of the Hunter squadron call 'Bingo' — the signal that he and his pilots were breaking off the friendly battle with the F-100s and returning to base, their fuel low.

Yeoman was the last to land, making a straight-in approach and setting the Hunter down gently just beyond the striped markings at the end of Sylt's long runway. He taxied to the end of the flight line, following the directions of a marshaller, and quickly completed his post-flight checks, shutting down the Hunter's Rolls-Royce Avon turbojet. He had taxied in with the cockpit canopy open, and now an airman came forward with an aluminium ladder, which he hooked over the cockpit rim. The airman climbed up and Yeoman handed him the safety pin for the top handle of the Martin-Baker ejection seat, which the man slotted into place; Yeoman himself inserted the second pin, which prevented the accidental pulling of the seat pan handle, between the pilot's legs.

With everything switched off and the 'bang seat' now safe, Yeoman uncoupled himself from the seat connections, handed his 'bone-dome' flying helmet to the airman and shinned down the cockpit ladder, jumping clear of the last two rungs and flexing his knees slightly as his feet hit the concrete. The airman, a corporal, grinned at him.

'Good trip, sir?'

Yeoman grinned back and nodded. 'Spot on. Had a bit of a tussle with an F-100, but shook him off all right.'

He made his way towards the 'line hut', as the Handling Flight building was known. It had always been his practice to exchange a few words with the ground crew; some pilots didn't bother, and that annoyed him. The ground crew worked like slaves and their perks were few, so Yeoman got them airborne as often as possible on a rotation basis in one of the Rheinbrücken Wing's two-seat Hunter T7 trainers or the Vampire TII 'hack' aircraft that was used for communications work. It all made for higher morale, and for a more efficient and closely-knit station.

At the door of the line hut, where pilots book in and out and sign the Form 700, the technical log that certifies that an aircraft is free from snags, Yeoman paused for a few moments and looked out over the airfield, revelling in the view. The sunlight sparkled on the grey-green camouflage of the long line of Hunters, looking sleek and potent even in their earth-bound environment. After the recent crescendo of high-powered jet engines, a silence that was almost unearthly hung over Sylt.

Somewhere, a lark trilled, just as it had trilled on that airfield in France on a day in 1940, so long ago, when Yeoman had first come face to face with the deadly reality of combat flying. He looked for the bird and found it at last, a minute speck hovering high above the tarmac.

The lark brought back memories to him, not all of them pleasant. A cold shadow seemed to fleet over him for an instant and he shivered despite the sun's heat. Something had seized him; a premonition, perhaps, or a vague sense of for-boding for which he could not account. It was still with him, like a chip of ice in his mind, as he went into the hut.

*

At Rheinbrücken, two hundred miles south-west of Sylt, it was also a day to remember; the kind of day that air-minded small boys recall for the rest of their lives, a day dreamed of and prayed for by anyone who has ever stood in pouring rain at an air display and striven to catch vague glimpses of aircraft fleeting through the murk.

There were a few scattered tufts of cloud here, but they were high and fleecy, permitting the rays of the summer sun to shine through unhindered, and the lightest of breezes was pleasantly cool on arms reddened by the heat of the previous days. But it was not the weather that had produced the day's magic; that had been created by the brutal noise of fast jets ripping through the sky, and by the smell of the kerosene fumes that drifted across the airfield in the wake of their passage.

A mild ripple of applause came from the crowd as four F-86 Sabre jets, bearing the iron cross markings of the Federal German Luftwaffe, touched down in immaculate formation at the close of their aerobatic display. The applause was hardly surprising, for the crowd was predominantly German. This was what the Americans would call 'Kids' Day' at Rheinbrücken; the RAF station had thrown open its gates to school-children from all over northern Germany in a major public relations exercise designed to strengthen relationships with the local community.

In the VIP enclosure, a much-decorated RAF Air Vice-Marshal paused in the act of raising a teacup to his lips and gazed at the Sabres as they rolled along the runway, losing speed. Even though it was fifteen years since the war had ended, he still found it difficult to come to terms with the idea of sitting in the sun on a German airfield, sipping tea, while a German crowd applauded German fighters.

Still, everyone was on the same side now, all part of that great multi-national defensive system called NATO, and after fifteen years the old enmities had disappeared. Anyone under the age of twenty who had been watching today's air show would be hard put to remember the war at all, and most of them didn't give a damn about the stories their fathers told them.

As the shrill whistle of the Sabres' turbojets died away, the Air Vice-Marshal turned to the woman who sat beside him. Rheinbrücken's commanding officer, he reflected, was a very lucky man indeed. His wife was in her early forties, but looked a good ten years younger; her figure showed no sign of approaching middle age, and the occasional undisguised thread of grey in the reddish-gold of her hair served to accentuate, rather than detract from, her beauty.

The Air Vice-Marshal took out a cigarette case and offered its contents to his companion. Smiling, she shook her head.

'No, thank you, Richard. I gave up ten years ago. Not good for the children to have the house filled with tobacco smoke, you know; George's pipe produces enough, as it is.'

Richard Fitzhugh Hillier nodded and lit a cigarette for himself. 'Very wise. Well, it's been a fantastic day, don't you think?'

'Wonderful. Do you know, in all the years I've been married to George, I think this is only the second air display I've seen from start to finish. In the past, I've usually been dashing round like a maniac making sure that everyone of importance had their cups of tea and sandwiches. Actually, I'm a bit cross with George for escaping to Sylt with all this going on.'

Hillier grinned. 'I'd have done the same myself. I don't much enjoy making small talk while other people are doing the flying, either.'

'Well, he hasn't shirked his responsibilities entirely,' Julia smiled. 'He's flying down from Sylt to do the solo aerobatic spot. In fact, he should be back in just a few minutes. He'll be pleased to see you again, Richard.'

Hillier was silent for a few moments. He was wondering whether to tell Julia about the real purpose behind his visit to Rheinbrücken. In the end he decided against it; there would be time enough for that later. He had no wish to spoil her day. Instead, he said, 'Your George has certainly come a long way since I first met him.'

Julia looked at him. 'Yes, but he's worked hard for whatever success has come his way. As a matter of fact, he has often spoken of you — about you being his first commanding officer in France, in May 1940, I mean.' She gave a mischievous smile. 'He said you were a stickler for the rules.'

Hillier raised an eyebrow. 'Did he, now? Well, perhaps I had to be, with unruly young beggars like your husband in my squadron. Those were bad times. There wasn't much room for individual heroics; we all had to stick together, or we'd have been in a real pickle.'

'Yes. It's hard to imagine, looking back over twenty years, just how bad those times were. All I seem to remember is the sunshine and the heat and the smell of flowers; I have to think really hard to recall German aircraft machine-gunning columns of helpless refugees. Maybe I've deliberately pushed all that out of my mind.'

Julia Yeoman paused introspectively, her thoughts turning to those far-off days when a chance encounter had first brought her face to face with George. They had both, in their respective fashions, been fleeing in front of the German 'Blitzkrieg'; he had been trekking west with a French refugee column after his Hurricane had been shot down when fate had overtaken the pair of them.

She would never forget her first sight of him, dusty and sweating, his RAF uniform dishevelled, standing in the middle of a French road with a small child cradled in one arm, the other raised imperiously to halt the French Army staff car in which she was travelling. She had been a journalist in those days, working at the Paris offices of the New York Globe, and had been visiting the supposedly impregnable Maginot Line when war had erupted on the Western Front. A senior French officer, glad of any excuse to be going in the opposite direction to the fighting, had offered to escort her to safety, but their car had become bogged down in a mass of refugees, panic-stricken after a German strafing attack.

The Messerschmitts' bullets had killed the mother of the little girl Yeoman held cradled in his arms when he stopped the car. Julia remembered how, in his halting French, he had asked for a lift to Chalons, to rejoin his squadron, and how the French colonel had flatly refused.

That had been his mistake, for Yeoman had promptly commandeered the car at pistol-point, regardless of the consequences. From that moment on, his fortunes and Julia's had been interwined, although — apart from a few brief periods together — the war had kept them apart for five long years. There were some things about Julia Yeoman her husband would never know. He knew, of course, that she had been an agent with the allied Special Operations Executive, and that she had spent terrible months in a Nazi concentration camp before her escape in the closing weeks of the war, but some things were best left unsaid. He would never know, for example, how many men she had killed; he was aware only of the nightmares that sometimes still caused her to wake screaming in the night. But they, too, were becoming less frequent with the passage of time.

Coming out of her reverie, she turned to speak to Hillier. At that moment, the airfield resounded to a sharp explosion, followed a split second later by another. Julia jumped, startled, and Hillier laughed.

'I think your husband has arrived,' he said. 'Look.'

Julia looked. High above their heads a silvery arrow streaked earthwards in the wake of the sonic boom it had created. Moments later, the screech of its passage reached them, a strident howl of sound separated from the aircraft by a tunnel of sky.

The Hunter came out of its supersonic dive, decelerating, and arced round the airfield, lining up with the runway. Yeoman began his display with a low, slow flypast, airbrake and landing gear extended, then cleaned up the aircraft and went into a tight aerobatic sequence that brought a buzz of approval from the spectators.

'He hasn't lost his touch,' Hillier said. Julia made no comment, although she felt a surge of admiration inside her as her husband brought the Hunter down for an immaculate landing, its wheels kissing the tarmac in a barely perceptible puff of smoke.

The display ended with a simulated ground attack run by twenty-four Hunters, blazing low across the airfield at high speed. Below them, explosives planted among 'enemy' vehicles, taken from a nearby scrapheap, detonated with a series of very satisfying bangs. Four Hastings transports from Abingdon, in Berkshire, dropped sticks of paratroops to mop up the opposition, and the crowds began to drift happily homewards.

A staff car took Julia and her guest to the commanding officer's house, a large and imposing building set among poplars some distance away from the rest of the officers' married quarters. Julia hated it; she had too many fond memories of the cottage she, George and the children had shared in Wiltshire.

Yeoman was in the shower when his wife and Hillier arrived, washing away the sweat of his aerobatic exertions. A knock at the bathroom door startled him, and the imperious voice of his daughter reached him through the hiss of the water.

'Daddy, mum's back, and she says you have to hurry up. You've got a visitor. And she says don't dare come down in just your dressing gown.'

Yeoman laughed. 'As if I would! All right, tell her I won't be a minute.'

He dried himself quickly, then went to the bathroom to slip on a clean shirt, flannels and sports jacket. He made a perfunctory stab at brushing his still-damp hair, proved quite incapable of dealing with an unruly bit at the crown, muttered 'to hell with it' and went downstairs, adjusting his tie.

Julia trapped him in the hall and gave him a long, searching kiss that held a promise of pleasant things to come. Disengaging herself, she said, 'Our guest is in the lounge, darling. I think he wants a word with you in private. I'm off to sort out what we're going to have for dinner and keep the kids out of your way. Off you go, now.'

She gave him a gentle push, propelling him towards the lounge door. He stood on the threshold for a moment, blinking in the golden sunlight that streamed in through the french window. A tall figure stood in silhouette, looking out into the garden. Yeoman, unable to make out who it was, came forward into the room, announcing his arrival with a cough.

'Good afternoon,' he said.

The figure turned to face him, right hand extended.

'Hello, George. You haven't changed much.'

'Good lord!' Yeoman, taken aback as recognition dawned, advanced to shake the other's hand automatically. 'Of all the people I expected to see, you were the very last, sir. Welcome! How long has it been?'

'Thirteen or fourteen years, I think,' Hillier said. 'When you were at Boscombe Down and I was at Staff College.'

They sat down and looked at one another for a few moments. Hillier lit a cigarette and Yeoman pushed an ashtray towards him.

'George,' Hillier said, exhaling smoke, 'this isn't just a courtesy visit. We might as well get down to brass tacks while Julia's out of the room. There's no need for her to hear what I have to say.'

Yeoman waited, chewing the stem of his unlit pipe. Hillier looked at him reflectively for a moment, then said, 'Four years ago, you did a very good job in the Middle East. In Muramshir, I mean. Averted what might have become a very tricky political situation in the Gulf.'

Yeoman still smarted over the episode. In 1956, he had been ordered to Muramshir, a tiny state on the Arabian Gulf, with two squadrons of Venoms, ostensibly to forestall an invasion by a powerful neighbour. They had, in fact, been little more than pawns in a high-level political game of chess; a game that had claimed the lives of several of Yeoman's pilots before it was ended. With some difficulty, he choked off an acid remark that rose in his throat and said nothing, waiting for what was coming next. Hillier did not keep him in suspense for long.

'Well, to cut a long story short, we've got another problem. You know about this business in the Congo, of course.'

Yeoman nodded. The recent tale of slaughter and atrocity in the former Belgian Congo, with rival tribal factions supported by foreign mercenary armies tearing that part of Africa to pieces, was known throughout the world. United Nations forces, drawn from parts of the globe as widely separated as Ireland and Nepal, were now campaigning to restore and maintain peaceful conditions.

'Yet another example of a former colony being granted independence before it's ready for it,' Hillier went on. 'Fortunately, it's the Belgians who have been suffering this time, and not ourselves, as happened in Kenya. Nevertheless, we are rather worried about the turn of events. It seems that one particular politician in the new Congolese Republic has been making good use of all the strife to consolidate his position as tribal overlord of a large slice of territory in the north-east of the country.'

'How does he concern us?' Yeoman asked, taking advantage of a brief pause while Hillier stubbed out his cigarette.

'Because,' Hillier explained, 'his territory is right next door to Warambe, where the British Government has a very definite interest. Warambe, you will recall, is a very small state that lies sandwiched between the Congo, Uganda and the Sudan. It supplies seventy per cent of our uranium, and naturally we don't want anything to interfere with that.'

'And you think this chap has designs on it?' Yeoman wanted to know.

'Yes, we do. His name, incidentally, is Nkrombe, and he seems to be quite a shrewd operator. He has surrounded himself with quite a formidable mercenary army, including a small fighter-bomber squadron equipped with F-86 Sabres, obtained from God knows where. We had no idea what was going on until a few days ago, when the Swedes told us.'

'The Swedes?'

'Yes. They form part of the UN peace-keeping force in the Congo,' Hillier explained, 'and are supported by a small air component. Until recently this has consisted of a few communications and light transport aircraft, but they've now got a couple of SAAB S-29C reconnaissance aircraft. The S-29C is a version of the Swedish J-29 jet fighter and is pretty fast, as well as having a long range. They are normally based at Leopoldville, but about a week ago one of them detached to Tanganyika to take a look at what was going on in the north-eastern part of the Congo. It photographed the area around Kerewata, which is the capital of the region controlled by Nkrombe, and got chased by a pair of F-86s. That was enough to make the Swedes sit up and take notice, because there aren't supposed to be any F-86s in that part of the world, and when they came to analyse the photographs their pilot brought back they spotted several more Sabres, very carefully camouflaged, on an airstrip near Kerewata. There also appeared, to be quite a bit of military hardware such as armoured cars in the vicinity.

'To cut a long story short,' Hillier went on, 'the Swedes recognized a possible threat to our little colony of Warambe, and thought we ought to know about it. The upshot is that we're sending a couple of battalions of troops to Warambe from Kenya for border protection duties, and a squadron of Hunters to support them.'

'The Hunters will presumably be drawn from the Gulf?'

Hillier shook his head. 'No. That's the problem. The two Hunter squadrons in the Aden Protectorate, Nos. 8 and 208, have their hands full in dealing with dissident tribesmen. The Hunters will have to come from the UK, but that's already in hand. As you are aware, 74 Squadron at Leuchars has been re-equipping with Lightnings for the past couple of months, and relinquishing its Hunter F6s; these have been flown down to the Hawker Siddeley works at Dunsfold for overhaul and some tropical modifications have been carried out. Eight of them are ready to go at this moment. Which brings me to my next question.'

'I think I know what it's going to be, sir,' Yeoman said resignedly. 'But do go on.'

'I want you to leave for Dunsfold tomorrow, George,' Hillier told him, 'and furthermore I want you and the Hunters to be *en route* for Warambe the next day. Your pilots have already been selected and the necessary clearances obtained. You'll be briefed more fully at Dunsfold by someone who is an old acquaintance of yours, or so I believe; a retired Air Commodore called Sampson. As I'm now involved in 2nd TAF Operations, he thought it only right that I should be the one to tell you. Didn't want to poach on my preserve, so to speak.'

Yeoman's heart was somewhere down in his shoes. Ten years ago he would have revelled in this sort of challenge; five years ago, even. But not any more.

'Why me?' he asked quietly.

'Oh, come along, George,' said Hillier testily. 'You're one of the most experienced combat leaders in the Service and certainly one with a lot of experience of special operations. You've liaised successfully with ground forces in Malaya and the Middle East; you know the ropes from every angle. You were the natural choice for this operation.'

'But I'm needed here,' Yeoman protested. 'We've a NATO air defence exercise coming up in a fortnight, and — '

Hillier cut him short. 'Your deputy can handle all that,' he said firmly. 'Wing Commander Roper is highly competent, and it will do him the world of good to step into your shoes for a while. Besides, we don't expect this present emergency to last for more than a few weeks; once the UN forces have established order in the central Congo they'll move up into the north-east, and that will be that.'

'Well, it doesn't seem as though I have a great deal of choice,' Yeoman said. 'Let me get you a drink. I could certainly use one. And then I'd better go and break the news to Julia. She isn't going to be at all happy about this.'

But fifteen years as a Service wife had conditioned Julia Yeoman into accepting whatever came her way without too much fuss. Yeoman came to her in the kitchen and, with his arms around her, quietly told her as much as he knew.

She managed a smile that was far braver than she felt.

'All right, George,' she said. 'We'd better make the most of tonight, then, hadn't we?'

And they did.

Chapter Two

THE ROUTE HAD BEEN CAREFULLY PLANNED. THE EIGHT Hunters would fly in pairs, with a fifteen-minute interval between each one, the first leg taking them from Dunsfold to Istres, in southern France. From there they would stage through Malta to El Adem in Libya, where they would top up their tanks for the long haul across the Sahara to Fort Lamy, in Chad. From here they could reach Warambe in one hop.

'We'll have to watch our navigation on this last leg,' Yeoman told his assembled pilots when he briefed them in a small room that had been set aside for the purpose at Dunsfold. 'The strip we'll be operating from in Warambe has only recently been completed, and as yet there are no radio aids. Moreover, it has been cut out of the jungle and is surrounded by mountains. If we find landing conditions impossible when we arrive overhead, we shall divert to Entebbe, in Uganda. On the outward flight we shall be preceded by a Hastings aircraft, which will drop off ground support parties at our various staging points, and another will follow us to pick them up again. Our spares, ammunition and so on are being flown down from Eastleigh, in Kenya.'

Yeoman looked at the pilots who sat in front of him in a semi-circle, scribbling scraps of information on the Perspex knee-pads of their flying overalls, and realized with a sudden shock that some of them were twenty years his junior. There were two exceptions; Squadron Leader Norman Bright and Flight Lieutenant Neil Hart, both Hunter men from 2 TAF in Germany, were in their thirties. Bright, a small, balding man who never drank alcohol — as Yeoman had discovered in the bar during the previous evening — had flown Sabres in Korea, on exchange with the USAF, and was very experienced. He would be a valuable deputy.

Yeoman completed his briefing and handed over to Air Commodore Sampson, who had been listening to the proceedings from a place in the corner. No-one but Yeoman knew who the grey-haired, slightly stooped man in civilian clothes really was, but his knowledge of the forthcoming operation was thorough and impressive, and left the pilots in no doubt that he was a person of considerable importance.

Yeoman's own involvement with Sampson went back as far as 1944, when the air commodore had been in charge of an Air Ministry department responsible for special operations. Yeoman had commanded a Mosquito squadron within the RAF'S NO. 100 Group, and had been assigned special — and usually highly dangerous — targets by Sampson's people. Their paths had crossed several times since then, most recently in the Muramshir affair of 1956.

Sampson's job now was to brief the pilots on the political situation in the Congo as far as it affected Warambe, and to answer whatever questions they might have. Predictably, they wanted to know the kind of opposition they might expect if they had to go into action.

'Nkrombe has assembled an air arm,' Sampson explained, 'consisting of about ten or twelve Sabres. That's more jet fighters than the United Nations have in the whole of the Congo. They are flown, as far as we can tell, by mercenaries, which means that some of them will probably be very good. Our Intelligence people are now at work trying to establish the identities of at least some of them, but it's not an easy task. However, we don't think that any former RAF personnel are involved, so at least that should give you a bit of an advantage.'

The remark produced some grins, but some of the pilots were wondering how the Hunter would fare in combat against an expertly-flown Sabre. So far, it had never been put to the test. Norman Bright had seen how the American jet fighter had performed against the Russian-built MiG-15 in Korea at first hand, and had come away impressed; it all depended on whether Nkrombe's jets were early-model F-86A Sabres or later F-86Fs, which could meet the Hunter Mk6 on more or less equal terms.

Despite his earlier misgivings, Yeoman was now quite beginning to look forward to the African adventure. He was in command of a first-class bunch of pilots and superb aircraft, and this time, Sampson had assured him, there would be no repetition of the Muramshir fiasco. The orders of the air and ground forces assigned to Yeoman's command were quite simple: to assure the security of Warambean territory in the event of any hostile moves from across the border.

Shortly before take-off, which was scheduled for 1000 hours, Sampson took Yeoman to one side.

'They tell me you're thinking of taking an early retirement,' he said quietly.

Yeoman was startled. As far as he knew, he had not voiced his innermost thoughts on the matter to anyone except Julia. He must, he told himself, have dropped a chance remark at some stage, and wondered how it had got back to Sampson.

'It had crossed my mind,' Yeoman told him.

Sampson looked at him thoughtfully. 'Then what will you do with yourself?' he asked.

Yeoman smiled at him. 'Nothing,' he said. 'Nothing at all, at least not for quite a while. I intend to walk the Yorkshire Dales, and fish, and generally lead the life of a gentleman of leisure for some time.'

'And grow roses, I suppose?' The question was slightly cynical, and Yeoman laughed. 'Oh, no, to hell with that. I never was a gardener. That's Julia's province.'

'Well,' Sampson said, 'when you've had enough of your walking and fishing, we might find something else for you to do. I'm looking for somebody to step into my shoes. Civil Service pay's not too bad, on top of your pension, and there's the odd bit of excitement. Think about it.'

'I've thought about it,' Yeoman told him. 'No, thanks.'

Sampson remained unruffled. 'We'll see,' he said. 'I don't think you're the type to take things quietly, not yet. In the meantime, good luck in Warambe. I'll be keeping an eye on you.'

Yeoman shook Sampson's hand and turned away with a nod, walking across the tarmac to his Hunter. He would be first away, followed by his number two, a quick-witted young Northumbrian named Peter Gibbons. The name had already caused some ribaldry, for the others had promised to introduce the youngster to some of his simian namesakes on their arrival in Africa. Yeoman had picked the young flying officer to be his wingman because Gibbons was not experienced in long-range flying; he had also paired up the others in similar fashion.

Yeoman and Gibbons lined up their Hunters on Dunsfold's main runway and opened their throttles in unison. The takeoff run was longer than usual, for each aircraft, in addition to its internal fuel, carried two 230-gallon drop tanks on its inboard wing pylons and two 100-gallon tanks on the outboard pylons.

They turned south towards the Channel in a steady climb, going up to thirty thousand feet to clear the busy air lanes, and Yeoman contacted France Military Control to clear their flight to Istres, north-west of Marseille. The Hunters, in fact, carried enough fuel to take them all the way non-stop to El Adem, but Yeoman had deemed it better to retain substantial fuel reserves in case of any sudden diversions.

Yeoman and Gibbons were still at Istres, enjoying what the younger pilot described as a 'decent cup of coffee', when the second pair of Hunters arrived, led by Neil Hart. Everything was on schedule. With the fuel uplift complete Yeoman and Gibbons took off again, this time for Luqa on Malta, the scene of so much bitter air fighting in the summer of 1942. The brazen sky over Luqa, and the heat, brought back many memories to Yeoman, most of them unpleasant. But there were sweeter memories too, of a girl named Lucia, who had consoled him for a time after the letters from Julia had stopped coming. He knew now, of course, why they had stopped, but he had never felt any remorse for his brief affair with the Maltese girl. It had been something precious to them both, during the brief weeks it had lasted, and he would never forget it. Neither, he hoped, would she.

From Malta they went on to El Adem. The Libyan airfield was deserted except for some transport aircraft and half a dozen Canberras detached from Cyprus on a bombing exercise. It had not, Yeoman learned, been especially successful, as the commander of the Canberra detachment explained. He looked extremely unhappy.

'Hit the target right on the nose,' he said. 'Beautiful. Then we turned for home and saw the *real* target. Christ knows what we bombed. I'm expecting hordes of irate Bedouin to come charging over the horizon on their camels at any moment, waving claims for damage to personal property.'

He was clearly inquisitive about the reason for the Hunters' presence at El Adem, but since Yeoman was his senior by several ranks he did not ask, and Yeoman had no intention of enlightening him. In fact, he was preoccupied with the next stage of the journey, which required careful planning, for the flight would take them over more than a thousand miles of featureless desert until they descended to their next port of call, the French airfield at Fort Lamy.

The eight Hunters rendezvoused at El Adem and the pilots spent the night there, retiring early to bed after a meal. For safety's sake, the crossing of the Sahara would be made in formation.

They were up before dawn, walking out to their aircraft in freezing desert air that caught at their throats and painted the Hunters' wings with a thin layer of rime. Yet within ten minutes, as the first pair of fighters thundered down the runway and the sun began to push its rim over the eastern horizon in a blaze of colour, the cold of the night had been dispelled.

Yeoman had seen many a desert dawn, but this was one of the loveliest. Below the Hunters, as they climbed steadily out over Cyrenaica towards their cruising altitude on a true heading of 205 degrees, the desert was a glory of red and brown and purple; the sun a golden ball drifting in a haze of green and violet. Soon, as the sun rose higher, all that would change and the desert would become a featureless sea of ochre, bathed in a stark brazen glare.

Yeoman, always with an eye for detail, looked over to the right, where a series of desert tracks met in junction a few miles from the Hunters' track. Close to that junction lay the oasis of Bir Hacheim, where the French Foreign Legion had held out for vital days in the face of repeated onslaughts by Erwin Rommel's Afrika Korps after the latter had destroyed a British brigade in the fierce tank battles of 1942, and broken the impetus of the German drive towards Egypt.

There were plenty of tracks, clearly visible from the Hunters' cruising altitude of thirty-five thousand feet, to mark the first hundred and fifty miles of the desert crossing, and clearly-defined wadis, the courses of dried-up rivers, also provided useful visual checks to the Hunters' progress. The accuracy of their track had been established early in the flight by reference to the radio navigation beacons at El Adem and Benina, but there would be no more radio aids until they got a position fix from the airfield at Largeau, in Chad.

Gradually, the tracks marked on the chart folded on Yeoman's knee began to peter out, and surface detail disappeared to be replaced by great sand-coloured tracts bearing the ominous words 'Limit of Reliable Relief Information'. This was the Great Sand Sea, the shifting desert that had swallowed many an aircraft without trace in the years since men had first begun to fly over the desert back in the 1920s.

Yeoman tried to imagine what it must have been like for those early long-distance pioneers, in their stick-and-wire aircraft with engines that were prone to all sorts of malfunction. For them, a forced landing in the desert had meant almost certain death, either from thirst or at the hands of hostile tribesmen. It had taken them days to accomplish the same journey that the Hunters, thirty years on, were taking only a few hours to achieve, spinning their vapour trails six miles above the great vastness at 500 mph.

Yet the huge wilderness was not entirely deserted. The quest for oil, the twentieth century's life blood, had brought men to these wastes, and their camps lay to left and right of the Hunters' track; tiny circles on the map bearing such names as Bir Bettafal, Oasis P4 and, cryptically, BP-KCA Rig. The aircraft that flew weekly supplies into these isolated spots were much closer in outline and performance to the pioneers' machines than were Yeoman's speeding jets. He wondered, briefly, if the men at the oil camps would hear the distant thunder of the Hunters' passage, and pause in their tasks to watch the eight arrow-straight contrails, spearing across the sky on their southbound course.

After about an hour's flying the horizon ahead was broken by ragged mountains. Yeoman knew, without looking at his chart, that this was the Tibesti Range, with peaks rising to eleven thousand feet and more. Libya was behind them now, and the Hunters' radio navigation equipment, switched to the appropriate frequency, was beginning to pick up faint signals from the homing beacon at Largeau. The signals grew stronger as the minutes went by, and the resultant position fix the pilots were able to obtain confirmed once again that they were on track.

Forty-five minutes later, having established radio contact, the Hunters began a slow descent to Fort Lamy, a former tiny airstrip expanded during the Second World War as a staging post for the vast amount of air traffic flying the trans-African route from the west coast to the Middle East. The runway was barely long enough to accommodate modern jets, but all the Hunters got down safely. Because of the restricted runway, however, they would have to make the last leg of the journey to Warambe with much less than a full load of fuel, otherwise they would never get off the ground.

It was cool at Fort Lamy, much cooler than it had been a thousand miles farther north. Thanks to the Hunters' dawn departure from El

Adem the morning was still young, and the pilots were able to enjoy a second breakfast in the French Air Force officers' mess. Most of the personnel at Fort Lamy, Yeoman discovered, belonged to the Air Wing of the Foreign Legion, units of which were operating in Chad to keep rebellious tribesmen in check. The Legion pilots were fit, tough-looking young men of high intelligence, enjoying the same pay and status as their counterparts in the French Army Air Corps. *La Legion Etrangère*, Yeoman thought, had come a long way since the days of Beau Geste.

Yeoman's main concern at Fort Lamy was to check the *en route* weather to the south. They were, he learned, likely to run through a belt of rain over the mountains, but there was also the comforting news that this ought to be behind them by the time they began their let-down to Warambe. However, Yeoman decided to split up the Hunters into pairs with fifteen-minute intervals once more, to reduce the risk of collision if they encountered really bad weather *en route*.

The RAF ground crew party who had been dropped at Fort Lamy by a Transport Command Hastings the day before looked a little the worse for wear, and Yeoman suspected that they had been entertained in some style by their French hosts. The Hastings had gone on to Warambe with the last of the ground parties. A word with the NCO in charge of the Fort Lamy party, an elderly flight sergeant, confirmed Yeoman's suspicions. The NCO, unawed by the fact that a group captain suddenly turned up and started talking to him like an equal, spoke quite frankly and with some astonishment about his drinking experiences with the Legion.

'There was this sergeant-major, you see, sir; adjutant-chef, the French call 'em. He was the only one in the NCOS' mess who wasn't friendly. Nobody seemed to like him very much — not among the older chaps, I mean. Then I found out why. The sergeant-major was actually a Frenchman, and the rest weren't. Just about every NCO in that room was German. And, d'you know what? Just about every one of 'em between the age of thirty-five and forty had been in the Waffen SS during the war. They were doing their third stint with the

Legion. Daren't go back to Germany, or they'd be arrested as war criminals. One of them told me there'd been a whole battalion of former SS men serving with the Legion in Indo-China, and that they'd been pulled out because they were too rough with the locals.'

'What about the sergeant-major, chief?' Yeoman wanted to know.

The flight sergeant looked puzzled for a moment, as though he had forgotten how the conversation had started, then said, 'Oh, him. He came swaggering over after a bit and challenged me to a drinking contest, that's all. It didn't last very long, because one of the SS blokes slipped something into his drink. He went over as though he'd been poleaxed. Then we all had a bit of a party.'

'I can well imagine,' Yeoman said. 'You'd better pray that the backup Hastings arrives to get you out of here before your French pal wakes up.' The flight sergeant grinned, deftly put the finishing touches to replacing a panel over the radio compartment of Yeoman's Hunter, and announced that all eight aircraft were as fit to fly as they would ever be.

'In that case, chief,' Yeoman said, 'We'll see you in Warambe. Maybe.' Grinning, he made a significant throat-cutting gesture with his index finger.

Many of the personnel at Fort Lamy turned out to watch the Hunters' departure. They seldom saw jet aircraft, apart from a few Mistrals — French versions of the elderly de Havilland Vampire, detached from bases in Algeria — because Fort Lamy was used mainly by piston-engined transport and communications machines, and by a few civil aircraft *en route* to destinations in central or east Africa.

One such aircraft, a twin-engined Cessna 310, stood some distance away from where the Hunters were parked. A man lounged against one of its wings, observing the activity as the Hunters were prepared for flight; a second man sat in the cockpit, its door propped open.

The man in the cockpit smiled in satisfaction. With the aid of his camera's powerful telephoto lens, he had managed to obtain an excellent shot of the officer who was clearly in command of the Hunter squadron, and of several other pilots too. It was always useful to know one's enemy. The Colonel would appreciate that.

The two men watched the Hunters take off, each pair of jets swinging south-eastwards towards the Congo and the rain clouds that now trailed in a grey fringe across the Dar Rounga hills. At last, the man in the cockpit leaned forward and tapped the other lightly on the shoulder.

'We had better go now,' he said. 'I want to get across those mountains before the afternoon turbulence sets in. We don't want to damage our cases of medical supplies, do we?'

The other grinned. He, like his companion, spoke with a South African accent.

'The Frogs certainly gave them a thorough examination,' he said. 'Their faces were a picture when they found out that we really were carrying medical supplies, with official Red Cross certification and all. It obviously never crossed their minds that we might be the contraband. The Boss sure did a good job in arranging our documents.'

Ten minutes later the Cessna taxied out and took off, its 'mercy flight' to a destination in the Sudan sealed and approved by the French authorities at Fort Lamy.

For twenty minutes it held a steady eastbound heading. Then, like the Hunters, it too swung southwards in the direction of the Congo.

Chapter Three

THE MAN THEY CALLED THE COLONEL STOOD IN THE DOOR-way of the clumsily-thatched shack on the edge of Kerewata's airfield and watched the Cessna 310 as it came slanting down to land through a rift in the rainclouds, its wings glinting in a shaft of sunlight. He nodded approvingly as the pilot made a curving, fighter-type approach to the runway and levelled the wings crisply, closing the throttles and dropping the aircraft like a cut flower a few seconds later.

In the aircraft's cockpit, the pilot obeyed the control tower's instructions and taxied across the waterlogged surface of the field towards the distant shack. He surveyed his surroundings with distaste.

'Christ, what a dump,' he remarked to his companion. 'No wonder they're paying us well. But where the hell are the Sabres we're supposed to fly? The place is deserted.'

The man next to him nudged him. 'Take another look, man,' he said, pointing towards the forest that all but surrounded the airfield. It was a few seconds before the pilot spotted what his friend had seen.

At intervals, cave-like recesses had been created in the forest by cutting down undergrowth and smaller trees. The branches of the larger trees wove together overhead, completely concealing from any prying eyes in the air the Sabre jet fighters that were neatly parked in each clearing.

'Clever,' the pilot said admiringly. 'This Colonel bloke seems to know what he's about. Seemed on the level when he first got in touch with us, and his money was certainly good, but you can never be too sure.'

'You know,' the other man said, 'this place reminds me of some of the fields we operated out of in Korea. Pierced steel planking runway, that sort of thing.'

'Yeah. Those were the days. Good old No. 2 Squadron, South African Air Force. Wish I'd stayed in.'

'They threw you out,' his companion reminded him mildly.

It was true. The pilot, who had been a lieutenant with a promising career ahead of him — knocking down two MiGs in quick succession after No. 2 Squadron had exchanged its ageing Mustangs for Sabres —

had been caught out selling government property to the South Koreans and dismissed after a rather unpleasant court martial. Since then he'd been around the world a couple of times, making a lot of money in one spot, losing most of it in the next — but always flying.

He brought the Cessna to a stop close to the shack, turning it into wind before shutting down the engines. The two men climbed down, their feet squelching in sticky mud. They both wrinkled their noses as the smell of the place hit them; a foetid mixture of clay, rotting vegetation and something that was suspiciously reminiscent of an open sewer.

'Welcome to Kerewata,' a voice said. It was then that they saw the man standing in the shadowy entrance to the shack. They recognized him at once as the Colonel, the man who had got in touch with them in Johannesburg a matter of weeks earlier.

'Come inside.'

He shook hands with both of them and they followed him into the hut. It contained a table, several chairs and a shortwave transceiver. Maps were pinned to the walls. The Colonel waved a hand, telling the newcomers to sit down. Once again, they were struck by his voice: sharp and incisive and American, like that of a West Point graduate, but with another slight accent behind it. It was this accent that puzzled the two South Africans, but the Colonel's identity was no business of theirs and they allowed their curiosity to rest there.

The Colonel did not waste words. 'Well?' he said, and they knew exactly what he meant. It was the Cessna's pilot, whose name was Piet, who spoke.

'It's true. The Brits have sent a detachment of Hunters to Warambe. They passed through Fort Lamy while we were there. We counted eight of them. Also he pointed a thumb towards his companion '— Jan here got some photographs. Some mug shots of some of the pilots, including the bloke in charge. Thought you might be interested.'

The Colonel nodded. 'Well done. I did not think that the British would react so quickly. However, it makes no difference. Eight Hunters can be destroyed on the ground, and we have the initiative. They will not make the first move. They will allow themselves to be attacked before they take action. It was always the same with them. And then it will be too late.'

He opened a box on the table, selected a cheroot and lit it, his gaze fixed all the while on Piet, who felt uncomfortable. The Colonel's eyes were like ice-cold blue splinters. They were the kind that did not tolerate even the thought of disobedience.

'When is the attack likely to be?' the question was hazarded by Jan. The piercing gaze shifted to him, and the South African mentally resolved to say 'sir' whenever he addressed the Colonel in future.

'Soon, my friend,' the Colonel told him. 'Very soon indeed, before the British have time to send large numbers of troops to Warambe. Nkrombe's native army is considerable, but it is poorly trained. Even with the help of volunteers such as ourselves it will be no match for regular British troops.' The two South Africans noted that he carefully avoided the use of the word 'mercenaries'. He clearly regarded it as distasteful.

'But sir,' Piet protested, 'even if we — Nkrombe's forces, that is — invade Warambe successfully, who's to say that the British won't mount an expeditionary force to recapture the place?'

The Colonel smiled and exhaled a thin stream of grey smoke. 'Because it will not be worth their while,' he explained. 'You see, the intention is not to invade Warambe and keep it. The intention is to mount a massive raid in strength and destroy the uranium mines. I shall explain later how this is to be done. But the object is to wipe out Warambe's economy at one stroke. Without the mines and its uranium exports, Warambe will starve. Its people will revert to savagery. No matter what the British do, they will be unable to redress the situation. Fools though they may be at times, they will not pour money and aid into a colony that is no longer of the slightest use to them. Then will be the time for the real invasion, which will be unopposed. The mines will be made to work again; it will take years, but that does not matter. They will be under Nkrombe's control, and Nkrombe, whatever his faults, has a keen eye to the future.'

'What sort of man is he, this kaffir?'

The Colonel's eyes blazed. 'Do not use that word again!' His voice was like a razor blade, and Jan flinched. 'Nkrombe is your master, just as he is mine — for the time being, until our job is done. He is a highly intelligent man, and a very wealthy one. It is the colour of his money, not the colour of his skin, that should concern you!'

Jan muttered an apology and embarked on a studious examination of one of the wall maps. The Colonel kept his piercing eyes fixed upon him for a moment or two longer, then relaxed.

'All right,' he said. 'Pick up your kit from your aircraft and go to your quarters to freshen up. I will send a man to show you where they are, and also the location of the mess hut. You can obtain a meal there at any time; we have a native cook permanently on duty.' He gave one of his thin smiles. 'The menu is limited, but wholesome. The cook is part Indian, so I hope you like curry.'

'Sir,' Jan said, getting over his admonition, 'when do we get to fly?'

'If the rain holds off, we'll check you out later this afternoon. The crew room is next door to the mess hut. Meet me there at three o'clock.'

He bent his head to examine some documents on the table in front of him, ignoring the two South Africans completely. It was as though they no longer existed. A little unnerved by his sudden change in attitude, they rose and went out into the sunlight.

'Bit of a queer bird, that one,' Jan muttered as they walked towards the Cessna to retrieve their bags. 'Wouldn't like to get on the wrong side of him.'

Piet agreed. 'Must be able to fly okay, though,' he commented, 'or he wouldn't have landed this job. Wonder who he really is?'

Behind them, through the open door of the hut, the Colonel surveyed their retreating backs and smiled to himself. He enjoyed throwing new arrivals off their stride, and had a good idea what was going through their minds at that moment. These two would be all right; he had their records in front of him, and no-one had ever found fault with their flying. However, he would be in a position to judge that for himself, a little later on.

He leaned back in his chair and lit another cheroot, gazing thoughtfully at the rising cloud of smoke. The two South Africans completed his line-up of twelve pilots. They were a mixed bunch, but good; the best that could be bought under the circumstances, at any rate. They included three Frenchmen, three Americans, a Spaniard, a Belgian and two Germans; all but the Spaniards had seen action at some point in their careers, but the Spaniards were experienced men with several thousand hours' flying to their credit, and he had no doubt that they would acquit themselves well if it came to a fight.

He sighed, suddenly remembering the old days with a touch of nostalgia. He had seen hard and bitter times during the Second World War, but nonetheless he would cheerfully have swapped everything to recapture some of them, and to relive the company of some of the comrades who had been swallowed up in the great fighter graveyard over Europe during those years.

Apart from one short break, he had never stopped flying since then. A succession of flying jobs in the United States had brought him a measure of security, and the chance to save substantial capital, but the call of adventure had proven too strong for him to endure a settled life for long. With his savings secure in a Swiss bank account, he had fought as a mercenary pilot in half a dozen revolutions in Latin America and had established a reputation for himself as a combat leader of high repute — or rather re-established it, for as such he had risen very close to the top of the fighter aces' gallery of fame during the war.

There was money — a great deal of money — to be made amid the smouldering fires of foreign wars, and there would always be a place for the mercenary, but mercenaries were no longer just thugs and adventurers. The middle years of the twentieth century had produced a new breed of skilled men who were prepared to sell their expertise to the highest bidder — or, in some cases, because they were prepared to risk their lives for what they considered a just cause in a foreign land. Mercenary pilots had fought on both sides in the Spanish Civil war, and had flown for Finland against the Russian invader in the winter war of 1939-40; more recently, in 1948, they had helped the infant state of Israel to defeat the Arab nations who were threatening her with extinction.

Those men had flown for an ideal, but in the Colonel's experience idealists could be dangerous. He had set out to create something much different: a first-rate flying unit composed of men who were prepared to fight and fly and kill because that was their best trade, and they were not content with any other.

Basing himself in a small and sympathetic Central American country, he had used a slice of his capital to set up what, outwardly, was a legitimate export and import business. It was based on a very simple supply and demand situation. Small nations, some of them in the grip of internal strife or threatened by external forces, needed warplanes. The Colonel undertook to supply them, and if necessary the men to fly them.

In the main, the aircraft involved had been elderly piston-engined types, mostly American and surplus to military requirements. There had been no shortage of volunteers to fly them, but he had been ruthless in his selection; only the best would do. His fees were high, but so was his reputation; he would not provide second-rate machines or crews. It was a formula that had worked well, and in five years he had become a very wealthy man indeed — but one for whom wealth counted far less than the prospect of action.

The shipment of ten North American F-86 Sabre jet fighters to the Congo on behalf of his latest customer, Nkrombe, was his most ambitious project so far, and one that promised to pay the highest dividend. He had supplied not only the aircraft and pilots, but ground crews as well, all on a three-year contract. By the time it expired, it was hoped that the first batch of Nkrombe's own pilots and ground personnel, now under training in Egypt, would have reached operational standard. The Colonel had his doubts about that, but it was none of his business. He would have fulfilled the terms of his contract to the letter.

Nkrombe could certainly find no fault with the aircraft the Colonel had acquired for him. The swept-wing Sabre jet, which was supersonic in a dive and armed with six 0.5-inch machine-guns, had wrought havoc with its Russian-built MiG-15 adversaries over Korea eight years earlier. In USAF service it had been replaced by the F-100 Super Sabre, and considerable stocks of surplus aircraft had found their way on to the market, for sale to 'friendly' countries. The ten machines now in the Congo had originally been purchased, with the Colonel's connivance, by an agent in Mexico for resale to Latin America, but they had never progressed beyond Panama. Dismantled and crated, the Sabres had been shipped across the Atlantic to the Spanish island of Fernando Po, off the west coast of Africa, where they had been re-assembled and air tested; Spanish officials, their pockets bulging with hefty bribes, had obligingly turned a blind eye. From Fernando Po, the Sabres, flying by night and equipped with underwing fuel tanks, had flown to Kerewata in one hop, arriving with the dawn. Their support equipment and munitions had reached Nkrombe's territory by other, more devious routes.

The Colonel, through long habit, never ate lunch, preferring several mugs of strong black coffee accompanied by a succession of his evil-smelling cheroots. After dealing with some routine administrative matters, he spent a couple of hours touring the airfield, inspecting the readiness state of the Sabres and chatting with the ground staff. The pilots, with the exception of the two newly-arrived South Africans, were absent, having been given leave to go to Kerewata. It was not much of a place, but it boasted a few sleazy bars and two even sleazier brothels, hangovers from the Belgian colonial days. Most of the pilots and ground personnel were conscious enough of their personal hygiene to avoid the brothels, but those who were not were subjected to stringent medical checks. On the Colonel's orders, anyone who failed to report a visit to one of the brothels was automatically sentenced to twenty-four hours in the 'can', a corrugated metal box that stood in the middle of the airfield. It was just big enough to accommodate a man in a crouching position, and a twenty-four hour spell inside it, enduring extremes of heat and cold, was enough to drive anyone to the verge of insanity. It had not been occupied lately, which was proof enough of its effectiveness.

At 1445 hours precisely, the Colonel went to the crew room near the control tower. The two South Africans were already there, kitting themselves out in flying overalls and 'anti-g suits'. These were inflatable girdles that hugged the pilot's stomach and increased his tolerance to the forces of gravity that were exerted upon his body during high-speed manoeuvres.

The Colonel nodded to the two men, without speaking, and put on his own flying clothing. Almost immediately, sweat started to trickle down his body, but it would be cool at high altitude. When he had finished, he gave them a short briefing.

'This will be a familiarization flight,' he told them. 'After take-off we'll turn on to 110 degrees and fly as far as the lake, here — ' he pointed to the feature on a map '— and then turn north to follow the river that runs through the forest from the mountains in the uplands region here. The river is the border with Warambe, and I want you to take a good look at it, paying special attention to the location of bridges and the terrain around them on the other side. We will be called upon to carry out air strikes there when the fighting starts, and I want you to memorize the lie of the land. I shall expect you to draw a sketch-map of the whole route when you get back here.' He gave them some additional information, including radio frequencies, then said, 'Stick close by me. I don't want you wandering off and straying over the border. Clear?' They nodded. 'All right, then. Let's go.'

A jeep took them out to their aircraft and they strapped themselves in, the two South Africans feeling an old familiarity return as they did so, like slipping on a worn and comfortable jacket. Two ground crew stood by each aircraft, and the South Africans noticed that in each case one of the men was a negro, presumably under instruction from his more experienced white counterpart. They seemed efficient, and well able to carry out the tasks in hand.

With the help of an external power source the Sabres' J47 turbojets started effortlessly. Taxiing checks were quickly completed, the ground crews removed the chocks and the fighters started to move as the pilots applied a little power. With the Colonel leading, the three aircraft rumbled out of their forest shelters and along the PSP taxiway towards the end of the runway. The latter was too narrow to allow a formation take-off and so the two South Africans held clear while the Colonel pointed the nose of his Sabre towards the clear patch that had been cut through the screen of trees at the far end of the long metal strip. Holding the fighter on its brakes, he opened the throttle to 80 per cent rpm, then released the brakes as power built up and advanced the throttle to the fully open position.

The Sabre accelerated slowly, and the far end of the runway seemed very close by the time flying speed of 125 knots was reached. Its nose well up, the fighter pounded along the metal surface and then wallowed into the air; a feature of the Sabre was that it never 'unstuck' cleanly, but once the Colonel retracted the wheels and flaps it accelerated rapidly.

He held the fighter down until the airspeed indicator showed 400 knots, then pulled up in a climbing turn, looking back over his shoulder towards the airfield. The second Sabre was just getting airborne and the third was beginning its roll along the runway. The Colonel reduced speed to allow the others to catch up with him and then all three set course eastwards in an immaculate 'V' formation, the Colonel noting with satisfaction the professional manner in which the two South Africans tucked themselves in beside his own aircraft.

There were rainclouds on the northern horizon, but they were a long way off, beyond the mountains, and in the meantime visibility was good. The Sabres climbed to twenty thousand feet and flew on over a dense green carpet of forest, broken here and there by the snake-like trails of fast-flowing streams; the streams themselves were often invisible, their passage marked only by a twisting dark line among the trees.

The lake that was the Sabres' first turning-point was clearly visible, a long, L-shaped strip of water that glittered in the sun. From the elbow of the 'L', a cascade of water plunged hundreds of feet into a valley and vanished among the forest. The lake was fed by a broad river that wound its way northwards; the Sabres made a gentle left turn and followed it, keeping it off their starboard wingtips. Far ahead of them, the mountains marched in a blue line across the northern horizon.

The Colonel was looking down at the river, at one of the wooden bridges that spanned it where it narrowed, when something sparkled in the corner of his eye. Raising his eyes, he scanned the sky on the other side of the river. With a skill honed by years of practice, he soon made out the silhouettes of two aircraft, keeping pace with the Sabres a couple of miles away at the same altitude. Even at that distance, there was no mistaking the identity. He pressed the R/T switch.

'We've got company,' he told his companions. 'Three o'clock, level. They're Hunters.'

'Shall we take a closer look at 'em, sir?' The voice was Jan's.

'No! I told you, your orders are to stay on this side of the river. Keep your eye on them, that's all.'

So the British were flying border patrols already, he thought, within hours of their arrival. He had not expected them to be so well organized. Perhaps he should have known better.

The Hunters escorted the Sabres as far as the northern foothills, as though attached by an invisible thread. Then, suddenly, the British jets turned hard to port, swinging round so that they were directly above the river on a reciprocal course. Their message was quite plain: it said KEEP OUT!

The Sabres turned too, heading back across country towards Kerewata. The Colonel was in a thoughtful mood throughout the homeward flight. Perhaps it would not be so easy to catch the British unawares, after all. He would have to carry out some revision of his war plan.

The jet fighters dropped into line astern as Kerewata approached, extending their speed brakes to slow down as they joined the airfield circuit. Making the final turn towards the runway at 140 knots, the pilots reduced the speed to 125 as they brought the aircraft in 'over the fence', decelerating by keeping the nose held in the air after the mainwheels touched the PSP to avoid wear on the brakes — a technique the South Africans had used as a matter of routine in Korea.

They taxied into their shelters and shut down the engines, unstrapping themselves and climbing down from the cockpits. Piet joined Jan by the latter's aircraft and nudged him.

'We were wondering about who this chap might be,' he said, quietly indicating the Colonel, who was talking with one of the ground crew. 'Well, maybe we can take a guess at his nationality. Take a look at his Sabre.'

Jan looked, and saw what his companion meant almost at once. Painted just below the Sabre's cockpit, thinly outlined in white against the dark green camouflage, was an Iron Cross.

Chapter Four

THE COMMANDER OF WARAMBE'S SMALL FORCE OF MILITIA, the Warambe Rifles, was an Englishman, although Yeoman was quick to sense that Colonel Henry Hoskins would never have held such an exalted rank had he remained a regular officer in the British Army, which is what he claimed to have been. His uniform boasted a row of campaign ribbons that spoke of war service in the Far East, but Yeoman accepted his tales of fierce action against the Japanese with a pinch of salt. Hoskins looked every inch the administrator, rather than the combat soldier, and that was probably the essence of it.

He regarded Yeoman over the rim of a glass of pink gin. They were standing in the bar of a small hotel in the township that had sprung up adjacent to the airfield; it served as a mess for officers and senior NCOS of the Rifles, and also for Europeans who were involved in running the uranium mines and organizing the country's export trade.

'So, old boy,' Hoskins said, 'I gather you caught sight of the opposition this afternoon?'

Yeoman nodded. 'We saw three Sabres, but they behaved themselves and stayed well clear. Has there been much air activity along the border?'

Hoskins shook his head. 'Nothing to speak of. An occasional flight during the past couple of weeks, but nothing to worry about. I don't think Nkrombe will start any trouble. In fact, I don't see what all the fuss is about. The Governor seems to have gone off at half-cock.'

Yeoman made no reply. The Governor of Warambe, Sir Humphrey Carter, had greeted the Hunter squadron on its arrival and had outwardly shown considerable relief that the RAF jets had been despatched so quickly. Yeoman could now appreciate the reason why, having talked to Hoskins for a while. The man was far from suited to lead troops into action; he had been in a backwater for too long. Anyway, Yeoman told himself, it was no longer a matter for much concern. The promised British troops would soon be arriving, and he would see to it that Hoskins was kept quietly out of the way, where he would not be a nuisance to anyone.

As though reading the RAF officer's thoughts, the florid-faced Hoskins suddenly leaned forward and touched Yeoman confidentially on the arm. Hoskins coughed a couple of times, surveyed Yeoman with his shifting, watery eyes that told of a system shot to pieces by gin, then said, 'Look here, old man, I'll admit I'm a bit worried. I've had things pretty well organized around here, you know. All this is a bit of an upheaval. Came quite out of the blue. First I knew of it was when Sir Humphrey told me yesterday that you were on your way and that you've been designated commander of all forces in Warambe. Bit thick, that. Mind you,' he continued hastily, 'I'm not saying that you aren't capable, or anything like that. It's just that — well, you don't really know how things are out here, do you? Might make the odd mistake, not knowing the terrain, or the people, if you see what I mean.'

Yeoman turned on his most disarming smile and lied horribly. 'But, Henry, I thought you knew. You'll be absolutely indispensable. An absolute right arm. I'm relying on you entirely to give me a proper briefing on everything.'

Hoskins, the wind taken right out of his sails, puffed out his cheeks.

'Oh, well, that's different, of course, old boy. Didn't mean any offence, or anything like that. Naturally, I'll give you all the help I can.'

Yeoman, his smile unaltered, said, 'Well, thank you, Henry. I was counting on you.' Then he plunged in the knife up to the hilt. 'We'll start with an inspection of your forward defensive positions on the river. At first light tomorrow morning, say. There'll be no problems, I trust?'

Hoskins reddened and started to bluster. 'Oh, I say, old chap, first light's a bit inconvenient. I mean, there's a bit of sorting out to be done, and — '

'First light, Henry,' Yeoman interrupted firmly. Hoskins glared at him, grunted like someone about to have an apoplectic fit, then mumbled his excuses and left the bar, saying that he had things to do.

Yeoman watched his retreating back with the air of a man who had just pulled off a bloodless coup, then turned and ordered another beer from the African barman, who was desperately trying to keep a straight face. Hoskins, it appeared, was not very well liked.

A few moments later several of Yeoman's pilots, including Norman Bright, came into the bar, and Yeoman stood them a round of drinks.

Bright took a drink of beer and looked at his commanding officer quizzically.

'What's going on, sir?' he wanted to know. 'I've just seen Colonel What's-his-name, the Warambe Rifles chap, driving off like a blue-arsed fly in a jeep and bawling orders at anyone in his path. Damn near mowed us down.'

Yeoman grinned. 'I think,' he said, 'that Colonel Hoskins is even now arranging for various key points along the river to be defended, which I'm prepared to bet they are not at this moment in time. In fact, there are a great many things about this set-up which fail to impress me.'

Bright nodded. 'Me too. I'm very worried about the fact that we can't disperse our aircraft properly. The only bit of hard ground apart from the airstrip is the apron in front of the control tower; they'll be sitting ducks in the event of an air strike.'

'Well, it's up to us to make sure that they don't take us by surprise,' Yeoman told him. He looked at his glass thoughtfully.

'The biggest problem is that we have absolutely no intelligence about what preparations are under way on the other side,' he said at length. 'When Nkrombe does start his troop movements, they'll be covered by the jungle and we won't know about them until it's too late.' He glanced sideways at the barman, frowned, then said, 'Look, we can't talk here. Let's find a quiet corner. There are one or two plans I'd like to discuss with you.'

They took their drinks over to an alcove, well out of earshot of anyone else in the room, and Yeoman told Bright what was on his mind.

'The Warambe Rifles don't seem up to much, if Hoskins is anything to go by,' he said. 'I'm working on the assumption that they would not be able to stand firm against a determined assault, so I propose to concentrate them along the river. They'll take the first shock of any attack, and if they are going to break I'd rather it was there than at some key position farther inland.'

'In other words,' Bright interrupted, 'you're planning to use them as a sort of early warning line?'

Yeoman nodded. 'Something like that. It's no use concentrating all our forces along the river, because even when the two battalions arrive from Kenya we won't have enough to cover the whole of the river line. So we'll put out the Warambe Rifles in a thin screen, with the task of raising the alarm if and when the attack comes. Once they've done that, they can bugger off as fast as they like. Our own forces will be in position astride every conceivable approach route to the airfield and to the enemy's main objective, the uranium mines.'

'Isn't it a bit risky, letting them get so far?' Bright asked.

Yeoman shook his head. 'I don't think so. As I've already said, we don't have the manpower to stop them getting across the river. So we'll let them get across and then suck them in towards our prepared defensive positions, where we shall stop them, cut their lines of communication and finally annihilate them. But we must keep our air power intact, at all costs, and that's going to be tricky. One point in our favour is that Nkrombe's Sabres are day fighters, so the chances of a surprise night strike are pretty remote; however, we can't rule out the possibility of a night attack on the airfield by saboteurs as a preliminary to the main event.'

'Well, perhaps Nkrombe will think twice, now that we're here,' Bright pointed out. Yeoman shrugged.

'Perhaps, but I doubt it. He seems to be a pretty determined character, by all accounts. I'm certain that he hasn't built up a mercenary army — not to mention the beginnings of an air force — just for reasons of self-defence. If you buy the services of mercenaries you tend to do things with them, such as attack your next-door neighbour, and that means Warambe. There's nothing on the other side of Nkrombe's territory but jungle and primitive villages. No, Norman, I think he'll attack all right, and I think it'll be soon. We have to be on our guard constantly, which is why I've given orders for armed patrols in the vicinity of our aircraft and stores, and for four pilots to be at cockpit readiness in two-hour shifts all the time. It will be a bit unkind on our backsides, but it's better than being caught napping.'

He glanced at his watch and gave a yawn. 'I'm going to turn in,' he announced. 'It's been a long day, and there's a lot to do tomorrow. I suggest you get your head down, too. I want you to come with me and Colonel Hoskins first thing in the morning. Better tell somebody to give us an early call, preferably with a cup of tea.'

Getting to sleep was not easy. It was raining, and the drops resounded on the hotel's roof with a noise like a thousand tap-dancers. It was also unbearably hot. Yeoman left the electric fan on at first, but it whirred and clattered so much that in the end he switched it off, preferring to take his chance with the heat. At last, lying naked on top of the bed, he dozed off.

He awoke suddenly to a deep silence and lay motionless, marshalling his thoughts, unable to recall for a moment where he was. The rain had stopped, and it seemed to be a little cooler. Then, as full consciousness started to return, he knew instinctively that there was something wrong, something out of place.

There was a strange smell in the room. A musky smell, hard to identify, compounded of human sweat and something else. There was a sound, too, such as a person makes when he breathes with his mouth open. It came from somewhere between the bed and the window, behind Yeoman's back.

Tensing himself, Yeoman rolled off the bed, placing it between himself and whatever unseen menace was in the room. It was pitch black, and he could not remember the exact position of the light switch. Conscious of his nakedness, which made him feel horribly vulnerable, he rose into a crouching position, trying to relax his eyes so that they grew accustomed to the darkness. There was a gentle draught in his face, coming from the window, and he knew that whoever — or whatever — was in the room had come in that way. Goose pimples stood out on his arms, and he felt the hairs of his body starting to prickle in fear of the unknown.

A black bulk launched itself at him across the bed. A stink of bad breath fanned his face sickeningly, and fingernails raked his shoulder as he jerked his head to one side. An iron-hard head butted into his temple, half stunning him, and he lost his balance, toppling on to his left elbow with his assailant partly on top of him. His attacker's body was covered with some sort of oil, reeking and pungent, that made it almost impossible for Yeoman to get a grip on him.

In desperation, the pilot brought up his right hand, index and middle fingers stiff and extended, and jabbed them at the spot where he sensed the intruder's face ought to be. He was lucky. The index finger made contact with the pulpy softness of an eye.

His attacker gave a short bark of pain and jerked back his head. Following up his advantage swiftly, sure of his target now, Yeoman slammed the heel of his hand brutally up beneath the other's chin. He both felt and heard the sinews of the man's neck crack and the assailant recoiled, falling back across the bed. Yeoman scrambled up and hurled himself towards the door, groping for the light switch, blinking as the solitary bulb flashed on in response to his command.

The room was empty. Like a cat, the attacker must have flung himself through the open window. Yeoman ran across the room and peered out into the night, but the man had melted away into the shadows.

Breathing hard, Yeoman pulled a bathrobe round himself just as footsteps sounded in the corridor outside his room. There was a knock at the door, and Bright's anxious voice. Yeoman opened the door and leaned wearily against the jamb. Several other people, alerted by the rumpus, were looking cautiously out of their rooms.

'What happened?' Bright wanted to know.

'Oh, nothing much. Somebody just tried to kill me, that's all.'

Colonel Hoskins came puffing along the corridor, incongruous in blue silk pyjamas. 'Spot of bother, old boy? Glad to see you're all right. Happens all the time, you know. Should have warned you. Those common thieves know better than to try it on with we regular inhabitants. Shot one of 'em stone dead, once.'

'I don't think this fellow was after my wrist watch,' Yeoman commented drily. His face smarted where his attacker's head had struck it, and there were red scratches across his shoulder. He turned to Bright.

'From now on, Norman, everyone is to sleep with his side-arm within easy reach. If there are any more intruders, shoot first and ask questions afterwards.' He prodded his scratches gingerly. 'I'm going to have a shower to try and wash that bastard's stink off me, then I'm going to get some sleep. Don't forget we've got work to do tomorrow. You too, Henry.'

An expression of annoyance, and what might have been anger, flitted across Hoskins' face. Yeoman failed to notice it; he was too preoccupied with the recent attack on his person.

It continued to worry him when, feeling anything but rested, he was awakened before dawn by an African member of the hotel's small staff, bearing a tin mug full of tea that tasted like sump oil. It had, at least, the effect of banishing any residue of sleep. Yeoman showered again, and felt better; then he went to the dining room to breakfast on fresh fruit and scrambled eggs. In the course of the meal he was joined by Bright and Hoskins, the latter looking surly and crumpled. Aside from a muttered 'good morning', his only comment was that he had 'laid on' a Land-Rover to take them on their tour of inspection.

Yeoman insisted on visiting the airfield first, to assure himself that all was well there; then, with one of Hoskins' African soldiers at the wheel, he set off with the colonel and Norman Bright to see for himself how well the river frontier was defended.

The road to the main crossing point on the river ran close to several villages, each of which was responsible for the upkeep of its particular section. In some parts the road was good; in others, little more than a dirt track that would have represented heavy going for any vehicle other than the Land-Rover. The track ran between tall grass and brush close to the villages, but farther away it was flanked by primeval jungle, rising dense and dark on either side. The huge trunks seemed grey and leprous, starved of light; through clefts in the jungle roof patches of sky glowed pink, reflecting the rays of the morning sun.

The African driver kept his headlights on, and their glare startled packs of flying monkeys that hurled through the greenery in search of their first feed of the day. Birds, mostly thornbills, flashed briefly through the lamps' rays, their harsh cries sounding above the roar of the engine.

In places, the rains had turned the track into clinging mud that sprayed up from the wheels. The driver seemed to take great delight in hitting the worst patches, like a small boy jumping in a puddle, gleefully shouting *poto poto* — which, Hoskins informed the two RAF officers, was the local word for something nasty.

After a two-hour drive, the jungle ended with an abruptness that startled Yeoman, giving way to a grassy plain that swept down in a long slope towards the river and the most important of its crossing points, a sturdy log bridge that was certainly strong enough to carry the weight of an armoured car. Hoskins ordered the driver to halt as the Land-Rover cleared the fringe of trees, clambered out and, panting with the exertion, broke some small branches from a bush. He handed them to Yeoman and Bright with the warning, 'You'll need those to keep off the tsetse flies. You'll always find the little beggars where there's water. You won't come to any real harm from them because you've had your jabs, but they can give you a painful bite. Gadflies are worse, but we aren't likely to run into them unless there are buffalo or elephant in the vicinity.'

After the damp darkness of the jungle, the sun-painted landscape that stretched out before Yeoman's eyes possessed an almost magical beauty. The placid water of the river was sandy-gold, its banks reddish in colour; on the far side of the bridge, the road shone white as it climbed towards a fringe of trees.

Close to the bridge, a group of Africans laughed and splashed in the water, their uniforms scattered on the river bank. Angrily, Yeoman turned to Hoskins.

'Are those your men?' The colonel nodded.

'In that case,' Yeoman blazed, 'what the hell do they think they're doing?'

Hoskins looked pained. 'Just having a bit of a swim, old boy. They've been hard at it all night, digging weapon pits, and — '

He broke off, reddening, suddenly realizing that he had just admitted what Yeoman had already suspected: that the river frontier had been completely undefended.

Yeoman looked at the foxholes dug by Hoskins' troops. They were sited haphazardly, and some were only half finished. They would have been quite easily overrun by a determined troop of Boy Scouts, let alone a determined enemy with mortars, heavy machine-guns and armoured cars.

Hoskins saw the look on Yeoman's face and strutted off down the bank, shouting orders. Reluctantly, his men broke off their aquatic activities and climbed out of the river, the sun glistening on their dark skin. They donned their uniforms and stood by their positions at some semblance of attention while Hoskins delivered a harangue.

'The sooner our regular units get here, the better,' Yeoman said to Bright. 'I don't give much for this lot's chances. It's a pity, in a way; with the right kind of leadership they would probably measure up. That fellow's about as much use as a chocolate fireguard.'

'That fellow' came puffing back up the slope, full of apologies.

'Lazy beggars,' he grunted. 'Got to keep your eye on 'em all the time, or they'll swing the lead. Be all right in a scrap, though. Brave as lions. Runs in the blood.'

Yeoman remained unconvinced especially when much the same scene was encountered at the next two defensive sites along the river. To all intents and purposes, the men of the Warambe Rifles were on holiday.

They were worse than useless, even in the role of early warning, which Yeoman had intended for them. The river line would have to be 'corseted' with men from the British force that would soon be arriving, even at the expense of depleting the main sectors.

Although they were completely unmilitary, the African troops were cheerful, happy-go-lucky souls, and in a way Yeoman's heart went out to them. By the time the Land-Rover reached the last defensive position, overlooking a ford at a spot where the river ran between high banks, it was noon and the men were cooking their midday meal in a black clay vessel that was covered in green leaves to seal in the flavour of whatever was inside. Hoskins told the others that the men were offering them something to eat: 'Better not refuse, chaps, or they'll be offended. Grin and bear it, what?'

A smiling soldier handed Yeoman a chunk of meat wrapped in leaves, together with some manioc which, he indicated, was to be dipped in some kind of sauce that another soldier was stirring in a large mess tin. Yeoman tried the meat first; it was whitish, like well-cooked pork, and had the flavour of chicken, although it was rather tough and chewy and fragments got stuck in his teeth. He asked Hoskins what it was.

'Python,' the other replied calmly, and was mildly surprised when Yeoman — veteran of more than one jungle survival exercise — showed no reaction and, instead, bit off another mouthful. The sauce that went with the manioc was a different story; made of peppers, it was a fiery mixture that caught at his throat and brought tears to his eyes.

Their meal over, they set off on the return journey to base, taking the same route. As they passed the various defensive positions, Yeoman noticed that the men seemed far more alert and businesslike, although whether this was merely for show he had no way of telling.

The jungle closed around them again. Weary now, hot and sticky, they spoke little, and Yeoman felt almost relieved when it started to rain, the big drops hissing down between the trees and pounding on the metal bonnet of the lurching vehicle, raising little puffs of steam as they evaporated. The occupants were soaked within seconds, but Yeoman knew that they would dry out just as quickly when the rain stopped. In the meantime, the sudden coolness was bliss.

The rain's attendant frustration, for Yeoman, was that it made it difficult to light his pipe, for the tobacco in the bowl was damp. He grinned at Bright, who was seated opposite him in the rear of the vehicle.

'Do me a favour, Norman,' he said. 'Lean forward a bit, will you, and help me shield my matches until I get this thing going?'

The two men bent forward to form an arch, their heads touching. The Land-Rover, negotiating a marshy patch, was almost at a standstill.

The burst of automatic fire crackled inches above the bent backs of the two RAF officers and sent sodden chips flying from the tree trunks beside the track. In a movement that felt like slow motion, but which was in fact an instinctive lightning reaction, Yeoman seized Bright and dragged him to the floor of the Land-Rover. They lay there breathing heavily, waiting for the next burst of gunfire, but there was no sound apart from the hissing rain and the cries of startled forest creatures.

'Got to get out of here,' Yeoman said. 'I'll unfasten the tailboard. When it drops, get out as fast as you can. Dive behind the biggest tree you can find. Check your revolver and make sure it's okay.'

Bright nodded, then said, 'What about the other two?'

Yeoman glanced towards the front of the Land-Rover, where Hoskins had been sitting beside the driver. There was no sign of either man.

'Looks as though they've gone already,' Yeoman said, cautiously reaching out to unfasten the metal toggles that held the tailboard in position. The board dropped with a metallic clang and Bright threw himself out into the mud, closely followed by his commanding officer.

Yeoman rolled clear of the track, scratching himself on some thorns, and took refuge among some tree roots, dragging out the Colt .45 pistol which he carried in preference to the standard issue Smith and Wesson .38. Out of the corner of his eye he saw Bright, jungle fatigues spattered with sticky mud, head well down behind a tree trunk. Apart from the cacophony of the jungle creatures, there was no sound other than the mutter of the Land-Rover's engine, which was still running.

Carefully, pistol in hand, Yeoman kitten-crawled towards Bright until he was in whispering distance.

'See anything, Norman?'

Bright shook his head. 'Not a thing. The shots must have come from over there.' He indicated a tangle of brush, some twenty or thirty yards off the track on the other side of the stationary Land-Rover. There was no movement from that direction.

Yeoman looked around, searching for some kind of support from Hoskins and the driver, but they were nowhere to be seen.

'Well,' he murmured, 'we can't stay here for ever. Look, do you think you can work your way along the track a bit? I'll do the same in the opposite direction. We'll be able to keep each other in sight. When I raise my hand, run like hell across the track into the cover of those big trees over there and I'll make for that clump of undergrowth to the left of the spot where you think the fire came from. If there is still anyone there, we might be able to force him out into the open. But mind how you go — and if you spot a target, make sure it isn't me. I'll be approaching from the opposite direction. And mind you don't trip over Hoskins. I've no idea where the silly bugger is.'

'Okay. I'm on my way.'

The two men began to crawl in opposite directions until they were separated by fifty yards or so. Yeoman halted and looked back; Bright's face was a pale blur among a screen of grasses. Taking a deep breath, Yeoman gathered his legs under him and, grasping his Colt firmly in his right hand, signalled to the other man with his left.

As though on springs, they both burst through the grassy screen that fringed the track and flung themselves across the few yards to the other side, their feet squelching in the clinging mud, bent double in fearful expectation of another burst of gunfire. It never came. Panting, his heart pounding with reaction as much as with the effort of his sprint across the road, Yeoman leaned against the wet bark of a tree trunk and gathered himself together.

Wiping rain and sweat out of his eyes, he peered round the tree at his objective, the patch of brush designated by Bright. In the background, the Land-Rover's engine still hummed.

Yeoman took a deep breath and dashed forward to the cover of another tree, from where he could get a better view of the target. Everything seemed peaceful. Through the rain he caught a glimpse of Bright, ducking behind a tree on the far side. The squadron leader was much closer to the brush than himself.

Suddenly, he saw Bright emerge from behind his tree and stand in full view, his revolver lowered, and for a moment he thought that his companion had taken leave of his senses. Then Bright looked up and waved at him, and his voice, deadened by the rain and the surrounding trees, reached him faintly.

'Come on. It's all right. Take a look at this.'

Still fearful of a trap, Yeoman went forward cautiously, his eyes striving to penetrate the gloom of the jungle. Nothing stirred, and he reached Bright unharmed. The squadron leader pointed at something that lay among the tangle of undergrowth.

'What do you make of that?' he asked.

The man was dead: there was no doubt about that. He lay on his back, in perfectly regimental attitude, legs together and arms by his sides. Across his chest rested the barrel of a British-made Sterling sub-machine-gun. He was dressed in drab, olive-green fatigues, the front of which was drenched with blood that still oozed sickeningly from a mouth-like gash just below the man's chin. He was an African, although his skin seemed lighter in hue than that of the local people.

Yeoman felt his spine tingle, and could not resist an urge to look over his shoulder. The rain-swept jungle stared back at him.

'Do you think it was Hoskins who did this, sir?' Bright said quietly, his gaze riveted on the dead man. Yeoman shook his head.

'I doubt it. I've a feeling he's on the other side of the road, somewhere.'

As though in response to Yeoman's comment, the portly figure of Colonel Hoskins suddenly materialized through the rain some distance away along the road, closely followed by the driver. The two of them made for Bright and Yeoman, in response to the latter's shout. Hoskins, Yeoman noted, did not seem unduly surprised to see the dead man but he bent down over the body and examined it thoroughly.

'Do you recognize him?' Yeoman wanted to know. Hoskins shook his head emphatically.

'No, old boy. Absolutely not. No idea who he is. Not one of our chaps, though. A deserter from across the river, perhaps. Good thing his marksmanship wasn't up to scratch, what?'

'Where did you get to?' Yeoman enquired mildly. Hoskins looked extremely embarrassed. 'Oh, well ... just decided to scout ahead along the road a bit, in case there were any more of the beggars about. Sound tactics, y'know.' He frowned. 'Can't think how the fellow came to have his throat cut, though. Bit of a puzzle, don't you think?'

Yeoman was forced to agree with him. 'Whoever did it must have moved very quickly,' he said. Bending down, he gingerly searched the corpse's sodden pockets, but they were empty.

'Nothing to say who he might have been. Do you think we ought to take him back with us?' Yeoman asked.

Hoskins looked more than a little horrified. 'Good God, no, old chap. Leave him here. The ants will make short work of him. There won't be a bone in sight by the morning. We'll take his gun, though. That's valuable.'

Hoskins retrieved the weapon and, without another word, squelched back towards the Land-Rover, followed by the others. For the second time in a few hours, the army officer's face wore a strange expression; the same expression that had fleeted across it immediately after the night-time attack on Yeoman the night before. Once again, Hoskins' features betrayed annoyance and anger, but this time there was a third ingredient. Fear.

Chapter Five

THE TWIN-JET ENGLISH ELECTRIC CANBERRA CAME slanting down from the north-east, its wings, caught in a shaft of watery sunlight, flashing silver against the dark green backdrop of Warambe's forested mountains as it curved in to make its approach to the airstrip.

Yeoman had just completed a stint of cockpit readiness when it arrived, and he paused, helmet in hand, to watch its landing. The touchdown was perfect, the pilot leaving himself plenty of space on the relatively short runway. The aircraft turned on to the narrow taxi strip, the note of its engines rising again to a shrill whistle as the pilot opened the throttles to obtain just enough power to keep the aircraft moving. It taxied in and was marshalled into position close to the line of Hunters.

The Canberra was the PR7 model of the famous jet bomber, designed for high-level photographic reconnaissance. It was uncamouflaged, the natural metal finish of its wings and fuselage being broken only by white squares, with the letters 'UN' painted on them in blue, where the national markings ought to have been.

Any curiosity about which air force actually owned the Canberra, however, was soon dispelled. The hatch in the fuselage side swung open and a man, presumably the navigator, stepped out. He wore a 'bone-dome' flying helmet, but the pilot, who followed him, sported a turban above a hawk-like face featuring a dark beard and a bristling moustache. As Yeoman approached, he noted that the epaulettes of the pilot's flying overall bore the rank insignia of a wing commander.

The fierce eyes took in Yeoman's own rank badges, and the pilot's hand came up to the turban in salute. Yeoman extended his own hand, smiling, and introduced himself. The other smiled back.

'My name is Ronald Engineer,' he said. 'An unlikely combination, but my great-grandmother was English and the male Engineers have had at least one English forename ever since. Tradition, and all that.'

The Indian Air Force officer's accent was fruitily English, with nothing more than a faint undertone of his native land. Yeoman guessed — and later had it confirmed — that Wing Commander Engineer was a product of the Royal Air Force College, Cranwell.

Engineer introduced his navigator, a flying officer named Sharma, and the three men walked together towards the flight hut while ground crew of the Hunter detachment busied themselves in checking over the Canberra.

'I had word that you were coming,' Yeoman said, 'although I must say I hadn't expected you so soon. I'm delighted you're here, though; we're desperately short of photo-reconnaissance, and indeed of all types of intelligence. I hope you can fill some gaps for us.'

The fact that the photo-recce Canberra belonged to the Indian Air Force came as a surprise to Yeoman; he had expected that an RAF aircraft would have been sent in response to his signal for help. Engineer clarified the position, telling Yeoman that his country would shortly be providing an air component to support the United Nations forces in the Congo; this would consist, initially, of four Canberra bombers, which would operate in conjunction with the Swedish J-29 fighter squadron. It would, he explained, be quite legal for his own Canberra to overfly areas of the Congo, for it would be doing so with United Nations sanction.

It was two days now since the episode in the jungle, and in the intervening period the Warambe defence forces had been substantially bolstered by the arrival of 500 men of the Cumbrian Regiment, flown down from Kenya. A further 1,500 were scheduled to follow. The first contingent was now deployed at strategic points inland, although a few had been assigned to the river line to keep an eye on the Warambe Rifles.

Yeoman felt much reassured now that the British troops had begun to arrive, but there was further reassurance, accompanied by another surprise, in the offing.

A couple of hours after the arrival of the Indian Canberra, two twin-engined Vickers Valetta transports landed on the airfield unannounced, except for a brief radio call requesting Group Captain Yeoman personally — and alone — to meet the leading aircraft. Mystified, Yeoman jumped into a Land-Rover and drove across the field to where the Valettas were parked, as far away as possible from the building and close to where the airfield perimeter was bounded by a strip of forest. As he drew up, he was just in time to see thirty or forty men, dressed in dark green jungle kit, disappearing quickly into the screen of trees.

Two men were standing by the nose of the first Valetta, awaiting his arrival, and he felt a sudden surge of pleasure as he recognized the shorter of the two. A lieutenant-colonel now, Christopher Swalwell looked no older than when Yeoman had last seen him; that had been four years ago, when Swalwell had commanded an SAS detachment in Muramshir.

Swalwell saluted and shook hands warmly with Yeoman, then turned to introduce the man at his side, a tall, sallow-faced individual who wore the red beret of the Parachute Regiment.

'This is Major Trevor Jones,' he said, 'who is to be my adjutant for the duration of this operation. He's known as Danglin 'Jones to one and all.'

'Danglin'?' Yeoman queried, and Swalwell grinned.

'His parachute got caught in a two-hundred-foot tree in Malaya once, and he was there for two days before somebody found him and got him down. His language, as they say, was choice. Isn't that so, Danglin'?'

'I was not amused,' Jones replied in a hollow voice. 'My balls still ache at the mere mention of it.'

Yeoman laughed and pumped Jones' hand. 'Well, welcome to Warambe, Danglin'. And it's good to see you again, Chris.' He pointed a thumb at the forest, into which the occupants of the two Valettas had melted like shadows.

'What are your hooligans up to?'

'Let's just call it "covert operations" for the time being,' Swalwell said. 'I'll explain in a bit more detail later.'

Yeoman nodded. 'Right. Just one thing, though. You'll shortly be meeting a chap called Colonel Hoskins. He's the officer commanding the Warambe Rifles, and he's a bit of a queer fish. If I were you, I shouldn't give anything away. I can't explain it, but I've an uneasy feeling about him.'

Swalwell looked mysterious for a moment, then said, 'Don't worry. I know all about Hoskins.' Abruptly, he changed the subject. Indicating the Valettas, he said, 'These chaps will be taking off again more or less right away. The crews are staying inside. All they want is to be topped up with fuel. Can you arrange that?'

'Of course. I'll have to fix it with the civilian establishment, because all we've got is AVTUR.' He named the kerosene-based fuel used for the jets. 'We'll call in at Air Traffic on the way over.'

During the drive back across the airfield, Yeoman told Swalwell and Jones about the two attempts on his life, and the mystery surrounding the demise of the second would-be assassin. Swalwell did not seem in the least surprised.

'There are obviously things afoot of which we know nothing,' was the only comment he made.

After making the necessary arrangements for refuelling the Valettas, Yeoman drove the new arrivals to the hotel in the neighbouring township where, after lunch, he briefed them on the current situation. Afterwards, he went into close conference with Wing Commander Engineer, and the two of them worked out the details of the forthcoming reconnaissance mission over Kerewata and its environs.

Engineer knew his business very well, as Yeoman soon discovered when the two of them pored over the available maps of the target area. The sortie would take place an hour after dawn, when the sun would be in a favourable position to cast shadows of any camouflaged objects on the ground; for maximum effect, the Indian pilot planned to make two runs over the target airfield, the first at twenty-five thousand feet. If there was no sign of opposition, he would make a rapid descent to fifteen thousand and overfly the airfield from west to east, diving to build up speed for the run home. To cover his retreat, Yeoman would put a section of four Hunters over the river at twenty thousand feet, but he emphasized that he would not be able to cross the river to intervene if the Canberra ran into trouble. Engineer was unperturbed, claiming that the Canberra could outmanoeuvre just about anything if it was properly handled.

Engineer and Sharma had few qualms about the sortie when they took off on schedule the following morning, climbing away to the east to reach the Canberra's operating height before turning on a reciprocal heading towards their target. Four and a half miles below, the river that separated Warambe from the Congo wound snake-like through folds of green and ochre.

Engineer headed straight for the target, which was not difficult to locate. A couple of miles from the airfield, the town of Kerewata lay shrouded in a mist of smoke from morning cooking-fires. The Canberra was rock-steady, only a hiss of air and the Machmeter reading of .7 betraying its progress.

The pilot completed his run at twenty-five thousand feet, continued on a westerly heading for some distance and then turned, extending the

Canberra's dive brakes to lose height rapidly. There was a slight buffeting as the Mach number increased, then Engineer levelled out at fifteen thousand feet to overfly the target in the opposite direction, cameras in action once more. This was the dangerous part of the operation, because the aircraft was flying directly into the sun; the light was blinding, making it hard to keep an adequate lookout. In addition, cloud was starting to build up around the target area, with billowing white cumulus tops already rising to the Canberra's height over to the left, beyond the town.

With the naked eye, Engineer could see no sign of movement on the airfield below, or on the roads that led to it; the cameras might tell a different story.

'Run complete,' he told Sharma. 'Very unexciting, really.'

A moment later, he could have bitten off his tongue. 'Forget I said that,' he told his navigator calmly. 'We have company. Two swept-wing fighters, three o'clock high. No, there are three of them, one some distance behind the other two. I think they are Sabres. Make sure your harness is good and tight.'

Sharma did as he was ordered, cursing the fact that from the navigator's position in the Canberra the view of the outside world was restricted. All he could do was sit tight, trust in his pilot's skill, and pray.

Quickly, Engineer called up Warambe on the radio and informed air traffic control what was happening. His message was acknowledged, so he knew that Yeoman's section of four Hunters would be taking off, if they had not already done so, to cover his retreat.

It was not going to be easy. Looking to his right, Engineer saw that two of the Sabres were heading to cut him off, black smoke trails streaming from their jet pipes as they increased speed, while the third was curving round to attack him from astern.

'Hold on,' he told Sharma. 'I'm going low, as low as I can. I don't want them to get underneath me.'

He stuck the Canberra's nose down and opened the throttles, sending a surge of power through the twin Rolls-Royce Avon engines. The airframe buffeted as the speed increased, and Sharma felt his ears pop as the Canberra plummeted downhill. From his vantage point in the pilot's seat, Engineer kept an eye on the two Sabres on his starboard beam and saw them start to turn in towards him; the one astern was still some distance away.

He levelled out a few feet above the forest, feeling a terrific sensation of speed as the treetops flashed beneath the Canberra's wings. The two Sabres were closing fast from the beam, but he kept the Canberra's nose pointed doggedly towards the sanctuary of the river, which was still a good five minutes' flying time away. Every few seconds counted; his timing would have to be as near-perfect as possible if he and Sharma were going to escape from this potential trap.

He risked a glance back and caught sight of the third Sabre, several thousand feet above and about a mile astern. Its pilot seemed to be making no move to attack; it was as though he were leaving the kill to the other two. The latter were now head-on silhouettes, their size swelling with frightening speed through the Perspex of the cockpit canopy.

Engineer's instinct told him when to act. With a fluid movement of stick and rudder, he stood the Canberra on its wing-tip and pulled the nose round towards the attacking Sabres, the 'g' forces crushing Sharma and himself into their seats. Levelling the wings again, he sped straight at the two jet fighters, which broke upwards to left and right, their pilots startled by the sudden manoeuvre. One of them fired a short burst, but his tracers went hopelessly wide of the mark.

Engineer swung the Canberra eastward again, its belly almost brushing the forest canopy. The two Sabres, carried on by their high speed, were away to the left and high, waggling their wings as they began to turn in search of their quarry.

The Canberra pilot made a lightning calculation. It would be anything up to sixty seconds before the Sabres were in a position to make another attack. The real immediate danger lay with the third Sabre, which Engineer saw was now diving from astern. If he held his present course, the fighter pilot would be presented with a straightforward no-deflection shot; it would be almost impossible for him to miss.

Ahead and to the right, and several thousand feet higher up, the base of a large cumulus cloud hung like a white cap over the apex of a hill that pushed its way up from the forest. Engineer knew that the cloud was his only salvation — if only he could reach it in time, before the three Sabres boxed him in and delivered the coup de grâce.

Once again he waited, ignoring the two Sabres which were once more running-in from the left and concentrating on the third, which had dived down to his own level and was closing rapidly. He knew that the Sabre was armed with six .50- calibre machine-guns; formidable weapons with a highly concentrated cone of fire, but weapons that made it necessary for the pilot to get in close in order to be certain of his kill. If the Sabre had been armed with longer-range cannon, he and Sharma would now be dead.

In his rear-view mirror, he saw the Sabre's nose suddenly light up with the flashes of its guns, and in that split second he heaved the Canberra into a turn to starboard. Pressure-induced contrails streamed from its wing-tips, and through a grey blur Engineer caught a dizzying glimpse of the treetops rotating beneath his right shoulder. His vision cleared and he reversed his turn, hurling the Canberra in the opposite direction. Over the intercom, he could hear Sharma's laboured breathing.

Engineer levelled out, and abruptly dropped the Canberra's flaps and dive brakes. The aircraft reared up, losing speed as though it had flown into an invisible barrier. Its pilot craned his neck, peering above and behind, and was just in time to see the dirty green belly of number three Sabre flashing over his cockpit canopy, its pilot having miscalculated his attack badly thanks to Engineer's sudden manoeuvre.

The Sabre pilot, an American who had destroyed four MiGs during the Korean war and who should have known better than to let himself be taken by surprise, swore at himself and turned away to make another attack. In doing so, he narrowly missed the two other Sabres, which were flown by the South Africans, Jan and Piet, and created momentary confusion.

It was Wing Commander Engineer's salvation. Cleaning up his aircraft, he applied full power and climbed hard for the cloud cover. Turning hard after him, the American was just in time to see the Canberra's angular silhouette swallowed up by the grey vapour. Without pausing for a second thought, only half hearing a cautionary warning that came over the R/T from one of the South Africans, the American also shot up into the cloud at a steep angle, the Sabre climbing at more than seven thousand feet per minute.

High above the cloud, which now extended across the eastern side of the frontier river, Yeoman, leading his section of four Hunters, heard

Engineer report over the radio that he was being attacked and was taking evasive action in the cloud. Almost immediately, he saw the twin-jet aircraft pop out of the white wall of the cumulus some three miles east of the river, turning slightly as Engineer got his bearings and headed for base in a shallow dive.

Yeoman pressed the R/T transmit button. 'Pearly One,' he radioed, giving the Indian Canberra's call-sign, 'we have you in sight at eleven o'clock, low. Will cover you.'

Engineer acknowledged, not troubling to disguise the relief in his voice, and looked up to see the four Hunters, diving down to guard his tail. He was not aware that he was still being pursued, but all four Hunter pilots saw the lone Sabre emerge from the cloud at the same moment, and Yeoman's warning call alerted him to the danger.

He had no cause to worry. The four Hunters split into pairs, one of which, consisting of Yeoman and Neil Hart, sped down to cut off the Sabre's line of retreat while the other pair arrowed in to place themselves between the attacking fighter and the Canberra. The American pilot, who now realized for the first time that he was on the wrong side of the river, saw the second pair of Hunters streak across his nose and turned hard to port to avoid them, intent on regaining his own territory.

The manoeuvre took him straight through the luminous 'pipper' of Yeoman's gunsight at a range of one hundred yards. A one-second burst was all that was necessary. Four 30-mm shells exploded on the Sabre's port wing root and the wing folded up, tearing away and whirling back in the slipstream. A fraction of a second before the fighter broke up and plunged into the jungle in a welter of burning debris, its transparent cockpit canopy flew off and a dark bundle ejected from the cockpit in a puff of white smoke. The ejection seat dropped away from the pilot; a yellow parachute deployed and floated down into the jungle.

Circling the spot, Yeoman made a radio call to base, fixing the downed pilot's position and calling for army units to search the area. He had no intention of allowing the mercenary pilot to slip through his fingers. The man would be able to tell him much of what he needed to know.

Returning to base, Yeoman placed all defensive forces in Warambe on a full war alert, anticipating the possibility that Nkrombe might use the shooting down of the Sabre as a pretext for launching a full-scale attack on his neighbour. But there was no doubt that the Sabre had been well inside Warambe air space; the wreckage was there to prove it. The remains of the fighter had been quickly located, but the day wore on and there was still no sign of the pilot. Yeoman knew, however, that he had escaped, because he had been careless enough to leave his parachute draped over the branches of a tree, where it had been spotted by a patrol. He would almost certainly be making for the river, and once he reached it it would not be too difficult for him to slip across under cover of darkness.

Meanwhile, as the hours went by, the fear that an invasion might be imminent increased, for the film brought back by Engineer revealed a convoy of what appeared to be armoured cars and trucks on one of the roads that led to a major river crossing point. At Yeoman's suggestion, the part of the Canberra's camera bay that was normally occupied by photoflashes was loaded up with standard magnesium flares; if a night attack developed, these would prove of invaluable help to the defenders.

Soon after dark, Yeoman, conscious that a busy night might lie ahead, went off to snatch a little sleep, and ordered those of his pilots who were not on standby to do the same.

He seemed hardly to have closed his eyes when he was summoned to the telephone by an RAF orderly. Bright was on the other end of the line.

'I think you should come over to the airfield right away, sir,' he said. 'We've got the Sabre pilot. He's in Operations; Major Jones is looking after him.'

Ten minutes later Yeoman, feeling wide awake now, strode into one of the rooms that had been set aside for operational use next to the airfield control tower. Bright was there, together with Jones and Swalwell, but it was the man who sat on a bench in the middle of the room who captured Yeoman's attention.

He wore a flying suit of USAF pattern, streaked with mud. His hands, unbound, rested on his thighs, and the fingertips of one of them drummed a nervous pattern. His face was square and dark-jowled, surmounted by a crew-cut, and it wore a truculent scowl.

'Has he said anything?' Yeoman asked. Swalwell shook his head.

'Not a word. He arrived in rather mysterious circumstances, though. About half an hour ago, our chaps who were guarding the main gate heard a commotion. Two men — at least, they think it was two, because it was hard to tell in the dark — ran out of the shadows and dumped something in the middle of the road, then they vanished again. Our men investigated, and the "something" was our friend here, trussed up like a turkey and with a hood over his head.'

'Well, well,' Yeoman mused, looking at the scowling prisoner. 'And he won't talk, eh?'

He walked slowly round behind the man and stood next to Jones, who was smoking a cigarette. He winked at the para-troop officer, took the cigarette from between his fingers, advanced a few steps and jabbed the glowing butt down hard on the back of the prisoner's right hand.

The man let out a yelp of pain and surprise and sprang to his feet.

'You goddam limey bastard, I'll take your eyes out!' he yelled. Swalwell hit him a sharp crack at the base of the throat and he fell back on to the bench, choking.

Yeoman coughed politely, hand over mouth. 'Well,' he said, 'at least we know his nationality.' He walked forward and stood in front of the man, hands clasped behind his back, and stared hard at him.

'I want you to know,' he told him in a voice that was barely above a whisper, 'that this limey bastard does not intend to mess around with you, and neither do the other gentlemen in this room.'

The prisoner coughed a couple of times and finally got his breath back. He stared at Yeoman murderously. 'I'm an American citizen,' he snarled. 'You can't knock me around and get away with it, you sonofabitch.'

Before Yeoman could reply, Swalwell stepped forward and stamped hard on the American's instep. As he jerked back in pain, Danglin' Jones hit him on the right shoulder with the edge of his hand. Something cracked.

'Don't cast doubts on the group captain's parentage,' Swalwell told him. The man groaned, clutching his shoulder with one hand and his instep with the other.

'You are a bloody mercenary,' Yeoman said, 'and as such I doubt very much whether your State Department will want to have anything to do with you. In other words nobody is likely to give a damn if you vanish off the face of the earth. Which is exactly what will happen to you, unless you start talking.'

The man groaned. 'The English don't do this kind of thing to people,' he muttered, as though to himself. Danglin' Jones gave a wolfish grin.

'Don't you believe it, boyo,' he said. 'And anyway, I'm not English, I'm Welsh. Nasty buggers we are. So be a good lad and spare yourself a lot of unnecessary pain. Tell us what we want to know.'

'After all,' Yeoman pointed out, 'it's not as if you'll be betraying your country, is it?'

Suddenly, the fight went out of the American. His shoulders slumped and he looked thoroughly miserable. 'Christ,' he said, 'you wouldn't believe I went through a year in a Chinese POW camp and never cracked, would you? Okay, I've got nothing to lose anyway, and I have no special grievance against you guys. My name's Cardwell. David G. Cardwell. What do you want to know?'

'Everything,' Yeoman said, 'beginning with Nkrombe's air power set-up. I want to know how many aircraft he's got, and who's flying them.'

'All right, but I can't give you exact identities. We all used pseudonyms, even the guy at the top. He's a strange bird. We just called him "The Colonel". It's my guess he's German, though, and a war veteran, because he has a little iron cross painted on his airplane.'

'Describe him.'

The American looked at Yeoman. 'About your height, I guess. Blond, close-cropped. Not a man to trifle with; very strict, but very fair too. And he can fly. Believe me, he can fly.'

Cardwell's eyes suddenly opened wide, as though in revelation. 'Is your name Yeoman?' he asked. The recipient of his stare nodded.

'Well then,' Cardwell said, 'the Colonel knows all about you. Some guy came up with a photo of you. The Colonel called us all together and gave us a special briefing. He didn't say how he knew about you — just told us who we were up against. You were one of the RAF'S top scorers during the war, weren't you?'

Yeoman made no answer. Instead, he put another question to Cardwell. 'How many aircraft?'

'Ten.' The American smiled ruefully. 'No, only nine now. All based at Kerewata airstrip. They're dispersed around the perimeter in jungle clearings.'

'I thought as much,' Yeoman said. 'That explains why they haven't shown up in our recce photos.' Abruptly, he changed the subject. 'Does Nkrombe really intend to invade Warambe?'

Cardwell looked startled for a moment, then said cautiously, 'We've been briefed to provide air cover for an invasion force, yes. But I don't know when the attack will take place. None of us was told that — just that it'll come sometime soon.'

Swalwell took a threatening step forward and the American winced in anticipation of another blow. 'Believe me,' he said, 'that's all I know. Why would I hold anything back? I'm not likely to receive any payment for my services from Nkrombe now, am I?' He suddenly looked very glum.

Yeoman nodded. 'All right. Leave him alone, Chris. I think he's telling the truth.'

Cardwell looked at him. 'What'll happen to me now?' he asked apprehensively.

Yeoman pretended to ponder the question. 'Well,' he said, 'I could have you shot, or your balls cut off, or something. Instead, we'll give you a feed and patch you up a bit — and then lock you away nice and securely until all this business has blown over. After that, I don't give a damn what happens to you. I expect you'll be turned over to the US authorities.'

Cardwell looked very unhappy at the prospect, and Yeoman briefly wondered what skeletons the man had locked away in his personal cupboard. Suddenly, he thought of something.

'One last question. Who brought you here?'

The American rubbed the back of his head. 'That's a very good question,' he said. 'This much I know. After being shot down, I lay doggo until dark, then set off in the direction of the river, following a road I came across. After a while I heard voices up ahead and assumed they belonged to a patrol, so I dived into the bush. The next thing I knew, somebody had me round the neck with a grip like a vice, and the muzzle of a gun was poking into my ear. Whoever the guy was told me to keep quiet, or he'd blow my head off. I didn't argue, not even when they blindfolded me and tied me up. Then I was thrown over the back of some animal — a horse or mule, I'd guess — and I don't recall much more until a little while ago. I was half suffocated and all the wind was knocked out of me, so I guess I must have passed out.' He paused and furrowed his brow.

'I can tell you one thing, though. I'll never forget the voice of the guy with the revolver. It was sharp, like the blade of a razor. And it was more English than yours.'

Chapter Six

THE MAN THEY CALLED THE COLONEL WAS NOT IN THE sweetest of moods as he drove down the bumpy road that led to Kerewata. It was not often that he showed flashes of intolerance, and he regretted the dressing-down he had administered to the two South Africans, Jan and Piet. After all, it was not their fault that the American had disobeyed orders and crossed the river to get himself shot down. He fervently hoped that the man was dead.

His thoughts went to another time, twenty years earlier, when he himself had been the target of bitter recriminations. That had been at the very outset of his career as a fighter pilot. It had happened on his first operation, when his lack of vigilance had resulted in two comrades being shot down. He had never forgiven himself for that episode, not forgotten the harangue delivered to him by his commanding officer in front of all the assembled pilots of his unit. After that, he had resolved never to criticize any of his own men unjustly; now he had broken that resolve, and felt the worse for it.

The narrow streets of Kerewata were filled with Nkrombe's African troops, lounging in groups and looking distinctly unmilitary. Nkrombe's residence itself was guarded by white mercenaries drawn from all parts of the western hemisphere. They were tough men, almost all of them former regular soldiers in some army or other, and although there were only about a hundred of them in Kerewata the Colonel knew that they would be more than a match for ten times that number of native troops. Events elsewhere in the Congo had already proved that.

Nkrombe's residence was a fine, whitewashed building of stone that stood in Kerewata's central square, impressive amid squalid surroundings. There was no wonder that it was impressive, for it had been built with foreign aid that ought to have gone to the relief of the people. The same aid, the Colonel knew, was paying for the services of the mercenaries in Nkrombe's employ.

The Colonel brought the jeep to a halt in the courtyard and made to enter the building, but was stopped by two heavily-armed mercenaries, who subjected him to a close scrutiny before allowing him inside. The procedure annoyed the Colonel intensely, for the men knew full well who he was. He knew, however, that it was pointless to protest, for the mercenaries were Belgians, as was their commander, and the latter had no love for anyone of the Colonel's nationality. It was ironic, for he no longer held that nationality, except in spirit; he had been an American citizen for years.

The conference with Nkrombe had been called for 1400 hours and the Colonel, as usual, was punctual to the second, a habit that never ceased to irritate his Belgian counterpart, who glared at him as he entered the conference room. The Colonel ignored him; it was Nkrombe who paid his wages. Nevertheless, he was conscious that the Belgian, the self-styled 'Brigadier' Koppejans, considered himself to be Nkrombe's right-hand man, and therefore privy to the African's secrets.

Nkrombe, resplendent in a uniform that would not have been out of place in one of the more humorous works of Gilbert and Sullivan, wore a displeased expression on his shining black countenance. He flapped a hand at the new arrival, indicating that he should sit down.

'I have news for you, Colonel.' As always, Nkrombe's speech was thick and slurred. The Colonel raised an eyebrow slightly and waited for what was coming next.

'Your missing pilot,' Nkrombe said, punctuating his sentence by tapping sharply on the table with a fly-whisk, 'is a prisoner. Let me say that I hold you directly responsible for his flagrant breach of orders.' For once, Koppejans showed complete satisfaction. Vaguely, the Colonel wondered how Nkrombe knew that the American had been captured. He must have an efficient spy network in Warambe.

'We must assume that he has talked to the British,' Nkrombe continued, 'in which case our plans may be in jeopardy.'

'But he does not know anything of any significance,' the Colonel protested. Nkrombe held up a hand for silence.

'He has been here long enough to know what forces we have at our disposal,' the African said, 'and he is therefore in a position to give the British much essential information. Once they know the strength of our forces, they will make an intelligent guess as to where, and how, we intend to employ them. They will doubtless, at this very moment, be deploying every available man along their river frontier defences.'

Suddenly, Nkrombe threw back his head and roared with laughter, his mouth a gaping pink cavern. Both the Colonel and Koppejans looked at him, startled, as he emitted guffaw after guffaw until glistening tears streamed down his cheeks. Then, abruptly, he rose to his feet and came round the table, still chuckling, to clap the Colonel on the shoulder.

'It was my little joke, my friend,' he chortled. 'Just my little joke. I am not angry at all. Really, I am quite pleased. Your pilot has unknowingly assisted my plan, not thwarted it.'

Koppejans looked thunderstruck, and the Colonel was not far behind him. He waited for the African to explain. Nkrombe was like a big, jovial child who had just sprung a practical joke on an innocent bystander — which, in fact, was not far from the truth.

Nkrombe's mirth subsided and he became suddenly serious. 'Come with me,' he ordered. 'Come with me, both of you, into the next room. I have something to show you.'

They followed him mutely, comrades for once in their mutual bewilderment. He opened the door of an adjacent room and stood on the threshold for a moment, arm extended as though indicating a new and unexplored terrain.

The room was empty except for a large table. On it was a relief model, meticulously constructed. The two Europeans peered at it curiously.

'My eldest son built it,' Nkrombe told them proudly. 'It took him many hours. See — it shows the location of Warambe's uranium mines. But it shows something else, too.' He laughed again. 'I can see by your faces that you are completely mystified, and perhaps a little in awe of my son's skill, yes?'

The Colonel and Koppejans exchanged sidelong glances which Nkrombe chose to ignore. Instead, he pointed to various details on the model.

'Look, here are the mines, in this valley at the base of a cliff.' His finger traced a path up the latter and crept over the summit until it halted at an almost circular feature, painted blue. 'This,' he explained, 'is the crater of a long-extinct volcano. As you will see, its walls form part of the cliff face; the crater itself has become a lake. It is not a big lake, but it is deep, very deep indeed.'

His face took on a triumphant expression. 'I have been clever, gentlemen. I have, as the English say, done my homework.' He paused for dramatic effect, then went on. 'There is in my possession a document, a document compiled by the British colonial mining engineers who first carried out a survey of likely areas of Warambe in search of valuable mineral deposits. It deals with the volcano, and the valley below it, in great detail.'

He turned again to the model and pointed out a thin white line which had been painted on the cliff face.

'This,' he told them, 'represents the position of a geological fault which runs through the cliff and up into the cone of the volcano. It is a weak spot, and I know how to exploit it. I have had expert advice. A few hundred pounds of explosive, detonated in the right place, will cause the fault to crack wide open and the whole cliff to split, right up to the cone of the volcano.'

The Colonel knew that Nkrombe was a highly educated man, but he had not bargained for this. Despite himself, he felt admiration for the way in which the African appeared to have worked things out down to the finest detail.

'Where is the right place?' he wanted to know. Nkrombe's finger retraced its path over the summit of the cliff and halted close to the base of the old volcano.

'Here,' he said. 'At this spot there is a chasm where the fault has opened out at the surface. This is where the explosive charges will be planted. When they detonate, water — thousands of tons of water — will pour down through the fissures from the volcanic crater into the valley below. The uranium mines will be completely flooded. No equipment on earth will be capable of pumping them clear. In time, the water will drain away, but it will take several years, and by that time it will be too late for Warambe. Long before, the Warambe Government will be seeking help from me, because it will not be forthcoming from the British. I will give it — but on my terms.'

Koppejans looked extremely annoyed that he had not been let into Nkrombe's secret. Nevertheless, he remained strictly polite.

'One thing I do not understand, sir, is why this action could not have been taken sooner,' he said. Nkrombe looked at him a little impatiently before replying.

'Because, Brigadier, it is one thing to know how to carry out an operation in hostile territory, but quite another when it comes to implementing it. I have no wish to invade Warambe; that is merely a facade. It is not necessary. I already have an army in Warambe — not a large one, but reliable nevertheless. It took time to assemble it — time and a great deal of money. People will do anything for money, will they not?' He looked directly at Koppejans, who showed no embarrassment at all.

'Then why build up a volunteer army if you have no need of it?' the Colonel wanted to know. He carefully avoided the use of the word 'mercenary'.

'On the contrary, Colonel, I do have need of it,' Nkrombe replied. 'There is a twofold reason. First of all, the British have decided that I intend to invade Warambe. As I have just explained, that is not true. Nevertheless, they have seen fit to strengthen Warambe's defences, which is a complication I had not envisaged. Therefore, in order for my plan to succeed — in other words, to enable my operatives in Warambe to carry out their task unmolested — it will be necessary to mount a diversionary assault at several points on the river frontier. The aim is not to cross the river, but merely to make the British believe that we intend to. Once the mines have been flooded, the diversionary forces can withdraw. There can be no fear that the British might pursue them across the river.'

Nkrombe folded his arms and his eyes took on a faraway look, as though he was seeing an inner vision.

'Warambe, with its mines — which will one day be workable again — represents my financial security for the future,' he continued. 'In the meantime, there are pickings to be had elsewhere. The whole of the Congo is in turmoil, and already several tribal leaders have asked for my help. It shall be given to them — but only, once again, on my terms.'

He looked at Koppejans and the Colonel in turn. 'With your help, I have made Kerewata strong, stronger than any other province in the Congo. Soon, when more of my own men are trained, it will be stronger still, strong enough to oppose the pitiful forces the United Nations are prepared to send into this part of Africa. But I do not propose to wait until the United Nations choose to confront me. I propose to act now, while they are fully occupied with the fires of revolutions that are sweeping through the land.'

His eyes blazed like black coals, reflecting a deep fanatacism, and he pounded a fist on the table, causing the model to tremble.

'This is why you are here,' he thundered. 'To form the spearhead of a force that will sweep west and south, rolling up the neighbouring provinces one by one and forcing their leaders to swear allegiance to me! Warambe is incidental — nothing more than a sideshow, at least for the time being. I will be to the Congo what Napoleon was to France! There will be a great empire here in central Africa, a black Empire, and I shall be its leader. I shall bring stability and peace to suffering peoples and they will remember my name for a thousand years!'

Suddenly, he lowered his voice until it was little more than a dull rumble, barely audible to his two listeners.

'Who knows?' he mused. 'With my empire secure in the west, who knows what the future may hold? Using Warambe as a springboard, I may even expand to the east. Uganda, Tanganyika ... perhaps even Kenya. Nothing is impossible.'

Koppejans coughed politely. 'I'm sure we wish you good fortune in your future ventures, sir,' he declared, conscious that he was lying, 'but what of the immediate plan concerning Warambe?'

Nkrombe returned to the present with a jolt. 'Ah yes, Warambe.' He smiled, flashing teeth stained yellow by nicotine. 'I almost forgot why I summoned you both here. All is now prepared, gentlemen. I have received word that the explosive charges will be laid and ready to be detonated within forty-eight hours. The diversionary attacks must be timed to start twelve hours before that. It does not give you much time, but time enough.' He smiled again, disarmingly this time. 'And rest assured — when my plans have reached their successful conclusion, the rewards for both of you will be greater than you imagine.'

The Colonel and Koppejans left Nkrombe's residence together. On the Colonel's suggestion, the Belgian agreed to come to the airfield to discuss details of air support during the diversions. For once, the differences between the two men were forgotten.

'You know something?' Koppejans hazarded as they drove off, 'I suddenly don't trust that fellow. He's a bloody lunatic.'

'No, he's not,' the Colonel answered. 'He's a man with fanatical ambition, which in a way is worse. Napoleon was one such, and Hitler another. They both failed in the end, but they dragged a lot of people down with them. Nkrombe will fail, too, but God knows what will happen in the process. He'll probably cause the whole of Africa to burst into flames.'

Koppejans was silent for a while. Then he said: 'What are we going to do? This whole bloody business is likely to get out of hand.'

The Colonel shrugged. 'He's paying our wages. The money is good, and we haven't been asked to risk our necks until now. I suggest we see this Warambe business through, and then make up our minds. If Nkrombe is double-dealing us for some reason, we must make sure that we are in a position to act first. We can always fight our way out, if we have to.'

Koppejans grunted. 'Wouldn't be the first time,' he observed. Suddenly, he looked across at the Colonel, who was driving. 'Look,' he said, 'just pull up for a moment, will you?'

The Colonel obligingly pulled the jeep over to the side of the road and halted, looking enquiringly at his passenger. With only slight hesitation, Koppejans stuck out his right hand.

'We've been at odds with each other ever since we got here,' he said. 'After what we've just heard, I don't think we can afford to be any more. So let's shake on it, and start afresh.'

'That's fine by me.' The man they called the Colonel took the proffered hand briefly, feeling pleased that the tension between himself and the Belgian seemed to be at an end. As they drove on, however, Koppejans had one further comment to make.

'There's just one thing,' he said, and the Colonel saw that he was grinning as he said it. 'I still don't like bloody Germans.'

The Colonel grinned back. 'Who said that I was German?' was all he had to say.

*

A deep, oppressive darkness fell over the Congo, bringing with it more rain. It lashed down on Kerewata, saturating the cooking-fires and the figures, huddled around them, of the troops who would soon be moving up towards the frontier with Warambe. The giant drops pounded with an unholy din on the tin roof of the shack at the airfield where the Colonel and Koppejans, surrounded by their senior officers, laboured under the pale light of generator-driven electric lamps to put the finishing touches to every detail of the forthcoming operations.

Elsewhere, the rain lashed down ferociously on the normally-placid waters of the river that divided the two territories, and here too men — British and African alike — huddled under their capes or whatever shelter they could find and cursed the sudden downpour.

Under cover of the rain and the darkness, shadows flitted silently among the trees, unobserved by any of the patrols or look-out posts. If a superstitious African had spotted them by chance, he would have been rooted to the ground in mortal terror, thinking that the shadows were jungle spirits. But they were men, and far more deadly than any spectre.

There were twenty of them. Like everyone else on both sides of the river they were soaked to the skin, but after three weeks in the jungle they were used to it and took it in their stride. For three weeks they had prepared for this moment, watching and waiting, and now their real task was beginning.

The men wore tight-fitting suits camouflaged with stripes of dark green and black, and fitted with hoods that concealed all but their eyes, so that even in broad daylight they would have been invisible against a jungle background. The back-pack that each man carried was also camouflaged in the same fashion.

Only in their weaponry did the men differ. Some carried machine-pistols, some carbines. One even carried a crossbow, a weapon as deadly as any rifle at close range and just as accurate in expert hands, with the advantage that it was silent. And the man who bore it was an expert; they all were. They all knew how to kill.

The men belonged to an elite special forces unit whose identity would never appear in any official document. It had been born in Malaya, during the early phase of the fight against the communist terrorists there, and had then held the title of Ferret Force. But once its purpose had been fulfilled, Ferret Force had been disbanded, and its men dispersed to other units.

During the years that followed, several of the men who had served with Ferret Force had mysteriously disappeared from the lists of the British Army. Some had been cashiered for various misdemeanours; others had simply vanished into obscurity. No-one, outside a certain small department in Whitehall, would ever have imagined that it was part of a carefully-orchestrated plan to form another unit composed of such men

— a unit so secret that its existence was not even suspected by the British Prime Minister.

During the years since its formation, the Special Force — it had no other designation — had operated all over the world, wherever drastic undercover measures were needed to safeguard British interests. The men who belonged to it were specialists in arctic, jungle and desert warfare, and all of them were fluent in at least one foreign language. Usually, they operated in small cells of two or three, but this time it was different.

Soundlessly, the men filtered down towards the river, reaching its bank at a spot guarded by men of the Warambe Rifles. The Africans were singing quietly to themselves, and the embers of a cooking-fire glowed through the rain, silhouetting the hunched figures of the men themselves. If an attack had developed from the opposite bank, they would have been sitting targets.

The soldiers certainly had no eyes for the twenty silent men who slipped by almost under their noses, and who waded out into the river until the water was up to their necks. The river was narrow at this point and the men swam across easily, their weapons strapped to the waterproof packs which they pushed ahead of them as they went. On the far side, the night and the rain swallowed them up.

The man who led the Special Force unit on its forced march through the dripping forest into Kerewata was no stranger to extremes of hardship and danger, but he knew that this would be one of the toughest assignments his men had yet been called upon to undertake. The brief of Peter de Salis, former army major and one-time commander of Ferret Force, was to kidnap Nkrombe.

Chapter Seven

THE GIANT, FOUR-ENGINED BLACKBURN BEVERLEY TRANSPORT aircraft came drumming down to land unheralded at the Warambe airstrip, landing in an amazingly short distance for an aircraft of its size. Yeoman, who was not exactly happy about unauthorized aircraft movements with Warambe on a state of full alert, drove out with Bright and a couple of armed soldiers to confront its crew. The wind was somewhat taken out of his sails when he recognized the first man to emerge from the huge aircraft's belly. It was Air Commodore Sampson.

'Good morning, Yeoman,' he said, as though holding a conversation over a cup of coffee in some civilized English drawing-room. 'Before you say anything, my apologies for the unannounced arrival. It was necessary to maintain radio silence, you see. I didn't want to advertise our presence to anyone who might be listening.'

Yeoman looked past the air commodore. The big clamshell doors at the rear of the Beverley's cargo hold had opened and various items of equipment were being unloaded. Sampson caught the direction of Yeoman's gaze.

'Don't concern yourself with that,' he said. 'The signals people are moving in. I want to keep in touch with various parts of the world without having to go through various laborious channels of communication.' He gave an unaccustomed smile as he noticed Yeoman's raised eyebrows.

'I know exactly what you're thinking,' he said. 'You are being kept in the dark, just like you were in Muramshir. Well, let me assure you that nothing from now on will happen without your knowledge, or indeed without your approval, since you are the operational commander here.' He laid emphasis on the word 'operational', and Yeoman was conscious of the fact that as of now, if there were major decisions to be made, it would be Sampson who would make them.

Cautiously, he said, 'I take it you have a further briefing for me, sir?'

Sampson nodded. 'Yes, but first some refreshment. It has been a thirsty flight.' He made as though to walk towards Yeoman's Land-Rover, then halted suddenly and faced the younger man.

'One other thing. The Beverley will remain where it is for the time being and no-one, no-one at all, is to be allowed near it without my orders.'

Yeoman had already noted a curious thing: several heavily-armed men, who looked as though they belonged to the Royal Air Force Regiment, had emerged from the Beverley and positioned themselves protectively around it. Why anyone should trouble to place a transport aircraft under heavy guard was a mystery to him, unless there was something very important inside it.

Later, in the seclusion of Yeoman's office, Sampson did nothing to enlighten him about the Beverley's contents, although he did bring him up to date on the situation in Kerewata. Things, Yeoman soon discovered, were not all they appeared to be.

'This operation,' Sampson told him, 'originally got under way following a request from our Foreign Office to safeguard Warambe's interests in the light of a probable threat from across the border. The threat still exists, but matters are no longer quite as simple as we had anticipated. Our operations here are now part of a much wider spectrum of activities, carried out under the authority of the Security Council of the United Nations.'

He placed his fingertips together and rested his chin on them, an old habit recognized by Yeoman as a prelude to some deep revelation. The air commodore continued: 'Let me explain the situation as Nkrombe sees it, according to our latest sources of information. First of all, his projected invasion of Warambe is little more than a sideshow, even though his intention is to neutralize the colony's economy by destroying the uranium mines. We are still not entirely certain how he plans to do this, although we have some indications.'

He paused, frowning a little, while Yeoman lit his pipe. Sampson was a non-smoker. Giving an exaggerated cough, he went on with his explanation.

'In his present situation, Nkrombe is a dangerous man. You see, he has an ambition to set himself up as some sort of emperor over a large tract of Central Africa. In other words, he is going full out to exploit the present turmoil. As you will doubtless appreciate, he has to be stopped.'

'Why not just have him bumped off?' asked Yeoman forthrightly. Sampson smiled, a little condescendingly.

'Ever the bluff Yorkshireman,' he said. 'That would be the easy way out, but it would lead to far more strife in the long run. We would be blamed immediately, and there would be a big outcry from several African states who, technically at least, are our friends. No, we have to be much more subtle than that.'

This chap, Yeoman thought, has more tricks up his sleeve than Professor Moriarty. He sucked his pipe and waited for whatever was coming next.

'Fortunately,' Sampson said, 'our plans are assisted by the fact that there are two separate factions in Kerewata. On the one hand there is Nkrombe's small regular army; on the other there are his mercenaries. We happen to believe that Nkrombe has made a big mistake in employing the latter, because feelings against the whites are running high throughout the Congo, and we know that some of Nkrombe's native officers are bitterly discontented about being compelled to take orders from foreigners. It was only the presence of the mercenaries that prevented them from joining in the mutiny of the Congolese Army a few weeks ago.'

'Perhaps that was why Nkrombe recruited them in the first place,' Yeoman interrupted. 'Perhaps he was shrewd enough to realize what would happen, once the Congo achieved independence from Belgium and became a republic.'

Sampson nodded. 'Yes, to some extent. We know that there is no love lost between Nkrombe and the Congolese Republic's prime minister, Patrice Lumumba; Lumumba has too many leanings towards his friends behind the Iron Curtain, and Nkrombe has no wish to be a puppet in a Soviet-controlled regime. There can be little doubt, now, that the mutiny of the Congolese Army was the result of a carefully-orchestrated plan; one just has to look at the quantities of Russian and Czech weapons and supplies that were flown into the Congo immediately after the mutiny to realize that. Lumumba, in fact, was jockeying for a position of complete dictatorship. Take a look at this.'

He handed Yeoman a typewritten document. He perused the wording, and realized at once that he was looking at relevant extracts from some sort of manifesto.

'Never be afraid of convincing people of our superiority or of inspiring imitation of us,' he read, 'for behind us we have a supreme power that will help us in anything whatsoever, with no hesitation. After other tribes are intimidated by our threats and shouting, we will be ready to submit them to complete domination. Do not forget that the white man is our enemy. Without him the Congo would already have been our domain, because during Arab times, our race had already ravaged several countries and had put them under our domination. The masses must be incited so that they never practice or believe the Christian religion, so that they can rebel against all the missionaries and priests more easily. It is very necessary to send our own people to all the universities of the world — the largest number of them to Russia, where they will have the most privileges.'

Yeoman looked up at the air commodore. 'What's this?' he asked.

'It's a document issued by Lumumba to his own tribe, the Bakusu, during the Republic's first elections,' Sampson replied. 'The underlying trend is very clear, isn't it?'

'Yes. But Lumumba has been deposed, hasn't he?'

'That's true,' Sampson agreed. 'He has been ousted by President Kasavubu, but he is still very much in evidence, even though Kasavubu is lined up with Mobutu, his chief of staff. Then there's the problem of Moise Tshombe, who has grabbed Katanga province for himself and declared it independent, in much the same way as Nkrombe controls Kerewata. It all adds up to confusion, murder and rape. You know what's been happening to the whites in the Congo, don't you?'

Yeoman nodded grimly. The appalling atrocities that had been committed during the mutiny by Congolese troops had caused a stir of revulsion throughout the world.

'But where exactly does Nkrombe figure in all this?' he wanted to know.

'I was coming to that,' Sampson explained patiently. 'Nkrombe, at the moment, is supported by the strongest mercenary force in the Congo and, as I have pointed out already, he plans to use it to establish himself as an overlord. What Nkrombe does not know, however, is that his own native troops are on the verge of revolt. The seeds of revolution have been sown among them, too.'

'Then that ought to be the end of everyone's problems,' Yeoman said. Sampson shook his head.

'Not a bit of it. You see, Nkrombe has the potential, with the right kind of schooling, to weld together the warring factions in the Congo. Don't forget that he is anti-communist, which counts for a great deal. Forgetting his aspirations towards Warambe for the moment, he has a great deal of potential as a valuable ally. If we allow him to be murdered by his own troops, it will destroy the one man we — and by "we" I mean the western alliance — can bring round to our way of thinking.'

'So what do you intend to do?' Yeoman asked.

Sampson looked at him for a few moments, then said, 'Kidnap him. Remove him out of harm's way. In that way we shall kill two birds with one stone. Our friendly African nations will applaud the fact that we took action to rescue an African leader from a bloody coup, and we shall be able to make a deal with Nkrombe once he is in our hands.'

Yeoman was dubious. 'It sounds a bit risky to me,' he said. 'For a start, how do you propose to get Nkrombe out of Kerewata? According to the American pilot we captured, he is very heavily guarded, both by mercenaries and his own men.'

'The plan is already being implemented,' Sampson told him. 'We have, at this moment, forces at work inside Kerewata. Their brief is to wait until Nkrombe's attack on Warambe is launched and his forces are fully engaged, and then go in and grab him. I think — '

He broke off suddenly as Yeoman raised a hand, placing the index finger of the other against his lips in a gesture of silence. Quickly, Yeoman rose to his feet and took a few silent paces across the room to the door. In one swift movement, he seized the handle and yanked the door open.

Hoskins stood outside, clenched fist raised as though he had been about to knock. He was red in the face, and had an evasive look in his eyes, like a boy caught in the act of smoking an illicit cigarette in the school lavatory.

'Yes, Henry,' Yeoman said quietly, 'what can I do for you?'

'Sorry to trouble you, old boy,' Hoskins blustered. 'Just thought I'd pay you a visit. Haven't had much contact with each other over the last day or two, and I really would like to know what's going on. Don't like not being kept in the picture, and all that.'

'You'd better come in, Henry,' Yeoman said, holding the door open. Hoskins stepped into the room and came to a halt, staring at Sampson, who rose and introduced himself before Yeoman had a chance to carry out any such formality. Yeoman noticed that he did not use his rank.

'I am very pleased to meet you, Colonel Hoskins,' Sampson said. 'We at the Foreign Office are not unaware of your valuable work in assuring Warambe's security. I take it your men are ready to meet the possible threat from across the border?'

Hoskins was taken aback by Sampson's suave compliment. 'Oh, why, most certainly,' he said. 'Brave as lions. Nothing to worry about in that direction, I can assure you.'

'Excellent. Now, if you don't mind, I do have a little business to discuss with Group Captain Yeoman. I shan't keep him long.'

Hoskins looked put out. 'Oh, very well,' he said, with a certain amount of ill grace. 'I'll see you later, Yeoman old boy. Catch up with you in the bar before dinner, if you aren't too busy, that is.' He made no attempt to disguise the sarcasm.

Hoskins left the room, and a few moments later they saw him pass by the window, accompanied by one of his NCOS. Yeoman looked at Sampson.

'There's something I ought to tell you,' he said. 'I don't trust that chap.'

'Neither do I, Yeoman, and believe me I have very sound reasons for not doing so. I hope he didn't overhear too much. Colonel Hoskins, I feel, is not all he seems to be.'

Yeoman removed his pipe from his mouth and regarded the other man directly.

'I get the impression,' he stated, 'that you know more about Hoskins than you are prepared to admit. Am I right?'

Sampson leaned back in his chair. 'Very well. I'll tell you this much. Hoskins is an impostor. In the closing months of the war he was a sergeant in the Army Pay Corps, stationed at Rawalpindi. There were, shall we say, certain discrepancies in the accounts, directly attributable to our friend. He was court martialled, spent a year in military prison, and dismissed from the Service. We have not yet worked out how he came to be here in Warambe; he was already in residence when the present governor was appointed, and the man's records were all in order. According to his personal file, he was a "hostilities only" man who came out of the army with the rank of major after six years of exemplary service. The record does indeed refer to a Major Hoskins who served in India — but he was posted as missing, believed killed, at Imphal in 1944. God knows how this chap got hold of the relevant documents, or how he managed to elaborate on them without being detected.'

'Good Lord!' Yeoman exclaimed. 'We'd better have him removed, right away.'

Sampson shook his head. 'No, that's the last thing we want. Hoskins is up to something, something big, and we need to know what it is. Let's give him plenty of rope and act as though we think he's genuine. He is under discreet surveillance, so he can't get up to much without us knowing about it.'

'This gets more complicated by the minute,' Yeoman complained. 'On the one hand there's this plot to kidnap Nkrombe, which I knew nothing about, and on the other there's the devious Hoskins, who isn't really Hoskins at all. Oh, yes, and there's an impending invasion, which is the reason for my presence here. Forgive me if I sound a little bewildered.'

'All three factors appear to be interlinked in some way, Yeoman,' the air commodore told him. 'And, insofar as your task in Warambe is concerned, that remains unchanged — except for one detail. Your Hunters may be required to fly in support of the special forces' group tasked with bringing Nkrombe out of Kerewata.'

'But, won't that mean operating inside Kerewata air space?' Yeoman asked. 'I thought that was contrary to orders.'

'Orders change, Yeoman, to suit the circumstances. You ought to know that by now.' Not for the first time in Sampson's presence, Yeoman felt as though he were back at grammar school, being lectured by his headmaster. 'As I explained earlier,' Sampson continued, 'we are now operating under the authority of the United Nations, so you will be quite within your rights to infringe Congo air space on UN duty. Which reminds me — you had better order your men to paint out the RAF markings on your aircraft and replace them with "UN" insignia. Do it now: you may have to go into action sooner than you think.'

Yeoman reached for a telephone and gave the necessary instructions. All the Hunters, with the exception of the pair sitting at the end of the runway on airfield defence readiness, would be sporting their new insignia before nightfall.

*

Fifty miles away, on the other side of the river, the Colonel was briefing his pilots. All Nkrombe's units, supported by mercenaries, were in position; the attack on Warambe's river frontier defences would begin at 0200.

The Colonel seemed a little disappointed as he spoke to his men, and it was not hard to understand why.

'Nkrombe's native troops,' he told them, 'have orders to cross the river at three points, here, here and here.' He tapped a map, laid out on the table around which the pilots were clustered. 'This is designed to give the impression that a full-scale attack is taking place, which, as you now know, it is not.'

He leaned forward, his hands on the table-top. 'Once they cross the river,' he went on, 'they will certainly be attacked by the British Hunters, starting at first light. It will not be possible for the British aircraft to strike before that, for they are day fighters, like our own Sabres.'

An expression of annoyance passed over his features. 'We ourselves are to patrol the west bank of the river in sections of three — one section on patrol, another *en route*, and the third ready to take off, so that we shall be providing constant air cover. Under no circumstances, however, are we to cross the river to engage the Hunters. Only if they penetrate our air space are we to attack them. Let us hope that they decide to take that risk.'

'Excuse me, sir.' It was one of the Germans who spoke. The Colonel looked at him questioningly.

'Are we to understand, sir, that our orders forbid us to give support to the Kerewatan troops, even though they may come under intense pressure?'

'You understand quite correctly,' the Colonel told him. 'The orders are Nkrombe's, not mine. I do not pretend to agree with them; my function is to obey them.'

He completed his briefing, then dismissed the men. The sun was already sinking. He had already ordered his pilots and ground crews to get a few hours' sleep before 0130, when they would be called to standby, and he intended to do the same, but first of all he had a call to make.

He was just in time. Koppejans was about to depart to take command of his men, who were encamped midway between Kerewata and the airfield. Twenty of them were already with Nkrombe's forces in the capacity of advisers; the rest, including Koppejans, were to take no part in the forthcoming action. Koppejans made it quite plain that he did not like the way in which his mercenary force had been split up.

'I don't like it, either,' the Colonel told him. 'I have a sixth sense that tells me when things are not as they should be, and right now it's giving me all manner of warnings.'

'Me, too,' Koppejans grunted. 'For a start, I thought that Nkrombe was planning to commit the whole of his native units to the assault on the river frontier, but there seem to be an awful lot of African troops still in and around Kerewata town. I ask myself why. I bumped into one of their officers earlier today, and he just wouldn't talk to me. Clammed up and walked away. I shouted at him, ordering him to come back, but he took no notice. Some of his men were nearby, and they started giving me some very funny looks. I mustered whatever dignity I could find and beat a hasty retreat, as they say.'

'Look,' the Colonel said, 'couldn't you quietly pull your men back here, to the airfield? I've a feeling we may need each other's support before long.'

Koppejans agreed immediately. 'All right. I'll filter them back in small groups, so as not to arouse suspicion.' He had a sudden thought. 'There are four of my boys guarding Nkrombe's residence, though. I'll have to leave them where they are, or it will give the game away.'

The Colonel shrugged. 'They'll just have to take their chance,' he said. 'Are you in radio contact with them?'

Koppejans shook his head. 'No, but I'll drive into Kerewata and have a quiet word with them. If there's the slightest hint of trouble I'll give them orders to get out as fast as they can, and to hell with Nkrombe. As you rightly say, there's something fishy going on. I'll fight like hell on anybody's behalf, so long as they pay me well for doing it, but I'm not going to be played for a sucker.'

They wished each other good luck. Koppejans climbed into his jeep and drove off towards Kerewata, stopping *en route* at the spot where his men were camped to have a word with his officers. Then, taking three of his more experienced mercenaries with him, he went on into Nkrombe's capital.

As they entered the town, they passed several army trucks parked by the side of the road. Some African soldiers were squatting close by. As Koppejans' vehicle roared past in a cloud of dust, one of the Africans rose to his feet, his eyes murderous, his hands clutching a machine-pistol. A colleague restrained him, placing a hand on his arm.

'Not yet, my brother,' he murmured. 'The time is not yet. Be patient. Before the dawn, the white dogs will be spilling their guts on the ground. They suspect nothing.'

He was wrong. As Koppejans drove on, he turned quietly to his companions and said: 'I was right. There is trouble brewing. Did you see the markings on those trucks we just passed? They belong to a unit which is supposed to be about to take part in the attack on Warambe. Make sure your weapons are cocked and ready. You never know what we might run into.'

Significantly, Koppejans noted, the streets of Kerewata seemed to be empty of civilians. Small groups of African troops stood at almost every street corner, displaying a vigilance which had been conspicuously lacking until now. Their eyes, almost without exception, showed hostility as Koppejans and his men passed by.

Curiously, there were no native infantry in the vicinity of Nkrombe's residence. Two of Koppejans' mercenaries were guarding the entrance; the others were inside, off duty. Koppejans called them all together and told them of his suspicions.

'Who's inside?' he asked, indicating the residence. The senior of the guards answered him.

'Nkrombe and his son, and the usual bunch of servants.'

'No African troops anywhere about?' The mercenary shook his head.

'No, none at all, as far as we know.'

Koppejans nodded. 'All right. Is your vehicle still okay?' He referred to the Willys quarter-ton command reconnaissance truck which the guards had at their disposal. It had a fifty-calibre machine-gun mounted on it. The guards confirmed that it was in working order.

'Okay, then,' Koppejans told them. 'Here's what you do. If there's any sign of trouble at all, grab Nkrombe and his son and bundle them into the Willys along with yourselves. Go hell for leather for the airfield. If you have Nkrombe and the boy, it should make the opposition think twice about trying to stop you.'

'And if it doesn't?' one of the guards asked grimly. Koppejans looked at him.

'I should have thought that would be obvious,' he said. 'Shoot the pair of 'em. You won't have anything to lose, will you?'

Chapter Eight

THE ATTACK BY NKROMBE'S FORCES BEGAN ON SCHEDULE at 0200 hours with a mortar barrage against several defended positions along the river frontier. The mortaring was not very accurate, and the defenders, who were well dug in, escaped with only three men slightly wounded.

Minutes after the initial bombardment, the men of 'A' Company, 2nd Battalion the Cumbrian Regiment, who were defending the main river crossing, were subjected to heavy machine-gun fire from the opposite bank. They kept their heads down and suffered no casualties, but a few moments later an armoured car trundled on to the bridge, the flashes of its cannon lighting up its squat bulk. It was followed by several groups of infantry, moving forward in short dashes.

'Let's have some light on the scene,' the company commander ordered. There was a brief delay, and then two flares popped into life high over the bridge, throwing the scene into stark relief. The armoured car, and the infantry, went on moving forward.

'They must be bloody mad,' said the company commander wonderingly. He tapped the shoulder of a man, a sapper, who crouched over a device next to him. 'Let 'em get halfway across,' he ordered. 'Hold your fire, everyone.'

The armoured car reached the centre span of the bridge. Its cannon barked again, and a 20-mm shell screeched over the British position to explode somewhere in the jungle.

'Now,' the company commander said quietly. The sapper leaned heavily on the plunger.

The centre span of the bridge erupted in a series of terrific explosions that lifted the armoured car bodily into the air. It fell into the river with a mighty splash, upside down, accompanied by a shower of screaming bodies and debris.

'More flares!' the company commander shouted. In their light, the British troops could see the dark shapes of men struggling in the water. Others were milling around on the far end of the bridge. For an instant, the company commander was tempted to let them go unharmed, then common sense prevailed.

'Open fire,' he ordered. Instantly, machine-guns sited along the length of the defensive position began to chatter, their bullets churning up avenues of foam in the darkened waters of the river, causing dreadful slaughter among the men who had survived the destruction of the bridge. It was all over inside thirty seconds; on the far bank, the groups of infantry who had been massing for the assault broke and fled into the night, while in the river a score of lifeless bodies drifted slowly downstream on the current. A handful managed to flounder ashore, wailing in terror. The machine-guns ceased firing.

'Funny,' the company commander remarked to his sergeant-major. 'You'd have thought Nkrombe would have used his white mercenaries in the main assault. That lot were Africans, and poorly-trained Africans at that. They did everything wrong, poor devils.'

The river frontier was now defended almost entirely by British troops, the Warambe rifles having been quickly assessed as worse than useless and pulled back to the rear. Communications between the various British units were excellent, and it was not long before information that began to filter through to the joint operational headquarters at the airstrip suggested that, although the attackers were being held at the principal danger points, small groups were attempting to infiltrate across the river at more lightly-defended spots. The Cumbrians' co came up on the VHF and spoke directly to Yeoman, requesting some air support.

Wing Commander Engineer and his navigator were already sitting in their flare-laden Canberra at the end of the strip, ready to go, and six Hunters were standing by. The Canberra had sufficient endurance to stay airborne over the river for several hours, if need be, dropping its flares wherever they were required, and the plan called for the Hunters to accompany it in pairs, each pair relieving the other when fuel ran low.

After take-off, Engineer and the two Hunter pilots in the first relay headed for the southern sector, a thinly-defended stretch where a British outpost had reported what seemed to be Kerewatan troops, equipped with collapsible boats, massing on the far bank of the river. The Canberra and the Hunters were overhead within minutes, just in time to catch the first wave of boats in midstream, making their crossing under cover of mortar and machine-gun fire.

Cruising over the river at five thousand feet, the Canberra released a clutch of flares that stripped away the darkness, revealing the surface of the water dotted with a score of dinghies. The two Hunters swept down to the attack immediately, their 30-mm cannon shells churning into the leading wave of small craft with devastating effect, the screech of their turbojets drowning the cries of men who suddenly found themselves lashed by a rain of high explosive.

Within seconds, the Kerewatan assault had collapsed in utter chaos. The survivors paddled as hard as they could for their own side of the river, harried by short bursts of machine-gun fire from the small group of British defenders. Overhead, the parachute flares dropped by Engineer sputtered and died out, plunging the area into darkness once more.

As the two Hunters flew back to base to rearm, Engineer radioed Operations to say that the enemy attack in the southern sector had been broken. He would continue to circle over the central sector of the river so that he could react promptly to any further calls for help.

Back in Operations, Yeoman and Swalwell were keeping minute-by-minute track of what was happening in the front line. Attacks were still in progress at various points, but they were not being pressed home with any great determination.

Yeoman, reluctantly, had decided not to fly in the night's operations, for he was needed to make on-the-spot decisions at the airfield. Engineer and Sharma appeared to be doing their work well, for in the space of an hour the Hunters made three strikes against targets on the river, all with success.

The Canberra's flare-dropping activities had not gone unnoticed in Kerewata, where the Colonel's small band of mercenary pilots were assembled at the airstrip in readiness to begin their patrolling of the river at first light. The Colonel was annoyed with himself; he ought to have foreseen that the British would have some such trick up their sleeve. As more reports came in, telling of the devastating strafing attacks that were being made by the Hunters by the light of the Canberra's flares, he determined to take some action.

Placing one of the other Germans in temporary command, he strapped himself into the cockpit of his Sabre and was soon airborne, climbing away towards the river. The Canberra, judging by the confused reports that were coming in, was dropping its flares from a fairly low level, so the Colonel decided to go high, flying parallel with the river at fifteen thousand feet. Far below, he could see the occasional flash of an exploding mortar bomb, and the flicker of tracers darting to and fro across the darkness.

Suddenly, a burst of white light almost dead ahead of him, and several thousand feet lower down, threatened to destroy his night vision. Blinking, he pushed the control column forward and headed towards the flare in a long, shallow dive. As he did so, three more flares burst beyond the first, forming an avenue of brilliance over the embattled river frontier.

In the Canberra's cockpit, Engineer and Sharma, their masked faces glowing in the dull red light of their instruments, were concentrating on making an accurate run so that the Hunters, orbiting off to one side, would have no difficulty in locating their target, three groups of infantry who had succeeded in slipping across the river and who now were digging in on the Warambe side. They were being engaged by the British troops, aided by the light of the flares, and Engineer quickly realized that the two forces were too close together for the Hunters to carry out a strike without serious risk of hitting their own men. He passed on this information to the Hunter pilots, who acknowledged and broke off their preparation for attack.

Seconds later, the Canberra's starboard turbojet exploded as a burst of .5-inch bullets tore into it. Shattered compressor blades ripped through the metal skin of the wing, and a terrific vibration shuddered through the airframe.

Engineer, who had no idea that he was under attack by another aircraft, thought that he must have been hit by ground fire. He yelled a warning to Sharma, telling the navigator to stand by for abandoning the aircraft, and immediately knew that they were too low. Sharma, unlike the pilot, had no ejection seat; his method of escape was to jettison the fuselage hatch and throw himself out into the airflow.

The pilot kicked the rudder pedals, slewing the Canberra round so that its nose was pointing towards friendly territory. At the same instant, he opened the port throttle, sending a surge of power through the good engine. The nose came up and the Canberra entered a roll, trailing flame and shedding fragments of wing as it went.

Engineer knew that he had seconds, no more, before the starboard wing disintegrated. The Canberra went over on its back and Engineer shoved the control column forward, raising the nose still further as the aircraft completed its crazy gyration across the night sky. The airspeed had fallen away dramatically, but the manoeuvre had gained a precious five hundred feet.

A blast of air entered the cockpit as Sharma kicked away the exit hatch. Engineer knew that he had sufficient control left for one more roll. Another few hundred feet would spell the difference between life and death for the navigator.

'Wait until I tell you!' the pilot screamed. Behind him and to the right, Sharma, who was still plugged into the intercom, acknowledged hoarsely and undid his seat harness, fighting against the centrifugal force that glued him to the side of the cockpit as the aircraft went into its second roll. This time, as the Canberra went over on its back, Engineer felt the controls go sloppy in his hands.

'Now!' he yelled, and glimpsed the dark bulk of Sharma's body silhouetted in the hatch before it tumbled out into the night. Almost instantly, there came a series of hammer-blows as the starboard wing started to break up. As it did so, the Canberra flopped over on an even keel, and it was this that saved the pilot's life; had it been otherwise, he would have ejected upside down, straight into the jungle.

He seized the seat-pan handle and pulled it with all his strength, blasting out through the cockpit canopy. Shocked and stunned, he had no recollection, later, of the seat dropping away and his parachute canopy opening.

Below him, and away to one side, the Canberra impacted in the jungle in a gush of blazing fuel. An instant later, its remaining flares exploded in a great ball of light that lit up the countryside for miles around. In it, with relief, Engineer caught sight of his navigator's parachute, floating to earth some distance away.

The breeze carried Engineer away from the thickest part of the jungle and he landed heavily at its fringe, breaking an ankle. Unable to walk, he stayed put until he was collected some time later by a British search party, which had also located Sharma.

The crash of the Canberra had been reported back to base by the two Hunter pilots who had accompanied it. Like Engineer, they believed that the aircraft must have been hit by ground fire, for they had seen no sign of any other aircraft in the vicinity.

Yeoman was delighted to hear that Engineer and Sharma had escaped with relatively minor injuries, but perturbed by the loss of the aircraft. Without its flare-dropping capability, it would now be impossible for the Hunters to carry out any further attacks before dawn, and by that time the enemy might have succeeded in pushing substantial forces across the river. Once they were swallowed up by the jungle on the Warambe side, they would prove extremely difficult to locate and eliminate. In the meantime, they might do an immense amount of damage, especially if they got near the airstrip. It all depended on how far the Kerewatan forces were prepared to go, and that was something only time would tell. The only thing to do, in the meantime, was to wait and hope that the defences on the river would hold against any major onslaught.

On the other side of the river, the Colonel, back at base after shooting down the Canberra, was also playing a waiting game. It was now 0345, and at any moment he expected to receive word that the operation against Warambe's uranium mines had been carried out successfully. After that, it would merely be a matter of pulling back the diversionary forces with the help of the air cover that would be provided by his Sabres.

What the Colonel had no way of knowing, however, was that the whole scheme was going badly awry.

*

In the shadow of the long-extinct volcano, it was pitch black, affording additional cover for the men who lay motionless under cover of the rocks that were scattered between the base of the volcano's cone and the cliff-top.

Fifty yards away, farther along the cliff, another group of men stood clustered around the geological fault that ran from the base of the volcano down through the cliff face. They were completely unaware of the fact that they had been under constant surveillance for the past two nights.

Major Danglin' Jones grinned in the darkness. It was time to bring matters to a head. The bait had been laid; all that remained now was to reel in the fish. He tapped the shoulder of the SAS trooper who lay next to him, and the man tripped a switch.

Instantly, the group of men by the chasm were bathed in the glare of a powerful searchlight that had been concealed among the rocks. They swung round, startled, and before they had the chance to get over their surprise a burst of machine-gun fire crackled over their heads. Some of them, in terror, hurled themselves to the ground.

Jones' voice rang out, and its authority and message were plain to the men of the Warambe Rifles, even though some of them knew no English. It was plain, too, to the white officer in charge of them.

'Don't move! Throw down your weapons, and no harm will come to you!'

Hoskins was on his knees by the chasm, fumbling with something on the ground. As Jones watched, a fuse sputtered into life. Hoskins sprang to his feet with remarkable agility, his round face sweating and triumphant, even in defeat.

'Do as I say!' he screamed. 'Pull your men back, or we're all done for! In ninety seconds this cliff will blow apart. None of us will stand a chance!'

The sparking end of the fuse vanished over the edge of the chasm. One of the Africans began to wail in fear and collapsed into a crouching position, head in hands, rocking back and forth. His terror was infectious; others of the group, apparently preferring to be shot rather than blown up, made a bolt for it. Sharply, Jones ordered his men to let them go.

Within seconds, all of Hoskins' men had deserted him. He stood alone at the edge of the chasm, trembling visibly as the seconds ticked away. The fuse was out of his reach now; he could not have extinguished it, even if he had wanted to in his desperation.

'For Christ's sake!' he cried hoarsely. 'We'll all be blown sky-high!'

'That's a chance we'll take,' Jones shouted. 'Make a move, and we'll kill you anyway.'

Hoskins, seized now by mortal terror, took a few shambling steps to his right. A light machine-gun chattered, throwing up a fountain of earth and stones at the terrified man's feet. He cried out and dropped to his knees.

The last few seconds ticked away. On the cliff-top, there was no sound except for the racking sobs that came from the huddled figure etched starkly in the searchlight's glare.

Danglin' Jones rose from his position behind the rocks and walked slowly over to the miserable Hoskins. Contemptuously, he prodded the man with the toe of his boot.

'All right,' he said. 'You can get up now.' Hoskins stirred, whimpering and Jones wrinkled his nose as a sudden stench hit his nostrils. Hoskins had fouled himself in his abject terror. 'Come on, you fat bastard, get up!' Jones ordered, his voice sharper.

Hoskins struggled to his knees and stared up at the para-troop officer, mouth agape. 'It didn't go off,' he stammered. 'Nothing happened. I'm alive.'

'That, unfortunately, is a fact,' Jones told him. 'And no, it didn't go off. Boxes filled with stones don't really explode all that easily.'

'Stones?' Hoskins shook his head in bewilderment, uncomprehending. Jones sighed. 'That's right, stones,' he said. 'You poor idiot, we've been watching you and your men stuffing that chasm full of explosives for the past two nights. After you'd gone, my chaps just lifted out the boxes, removed the stuff that goes bang, replaced it with stones and then put the boxes back again.'

Hoskins recovered some of his composure, and the tone of his voice showed ebullience. 'Why did you wait 'til now?' he snarled. 'If you've been spying on me for two nights, why didn't you spring your little surprise earlier?'

Jones grinned. 'I never have liked springing surprises too soon,' he said. 'Wanted to catch you in the act of lighting the fuse.' He gave Hoskins a sharp kick in the ribs. 'Now, get on your feet. There are people at HQ who would like a word with you.'

Leaving his men to round up Hoskins' fleeing accomplices, Jones, accompanied by an NCO, shepherded his prisoner along the steep track that wound its way down the cliff face to the valley below. A Land-Rover, summoned by radio, was waiting for them, and a fast drive through the night brought them to the airfield. The sky was growing light by the time they arrived.

Yeoman was in Operations, together with Swalwell and Sampson, when Jones shoved the blubbery Hoskins through the door.

'Got 'im,' Jones said simply.

'So I see,' Yeoman commented. 'God, he stinks. You might have cleaned him up a bit first. Open a window, somebody.'

He looked at Hoskins, feeling sympathy despite himself for the abject figure.

'What made you do it?' he asked quietly. 'We know about your background, but that doesn't matter. You had a good position here, and you were trusted. So why?'

'Money, of course,' Hoskins commented miserably. 'A lot of money. A million pounds in gold, to be exact.'

'Is that what Nkrombe promised you?' Yeoman wanted to know. The other nodded.

'It was more than just a promise. He let me have an advance, a big one. I needed to recruit men, you see. Fifty pounds was more than most of them had seen in a lifetime. They came over to my side without much trouble.'

'So it was your men who tried to kill me?' Again, Hoskins nodded, barely perceptibly. 'Yes. I hadn't reckoned with you being sent here. I thought that if I had you killed, it might cause just enough confusion to let me carry out my plan — or rather Nkrombe's plan — and get away with it. But things went wrong.'

'You can say that again,' Yeoman said. 'What did you do with the rest of the money you received? If you tell me you dished it out to your renegade troops, I just won't believe you.'

A flash of triumph came into Hoskins' eyes, and vanished just as quickly.

'It's where nobody can touch it,' he said. 'No matter what you do to me, short of killing me, you can't stop be being a very rich man one day.'

'We know where your money is, Hoskins,' Sampson com-merited drily. 'It's in a Swiss account, and you're right — nobody can touch it but you. You can use some of it to buy yourself a wheelchair when you come out of prison, because that's what you'll be travelling in. You'll be put away for a long time, a very long time indeed. Then again,' he added thoughtfully, 'you might not survive for very long in a Warambe jail.'

Hoskins blanched, and his eyes now showed naked fear. 'What do you mean, a Warambe jail?' he stuttered. 'For God's sake, you can't do that to me. I'm a British citizen. I'll be sent for trial in England, and — '

'No, you won't,' Sampson interrupted. 'You are a servant of the colonial administration of Warambe, so you will be court martialled here. You are a traitor, and as such deserve to be executed, but that would be far too merciful an end for you. A lengthy prison sentence will be far more appropriate. After all, the jail in Warambe is full of former acquaintances of yours. Doubtless you will have a great deal to talk about.'

Hoskins' face was a picture. What Sampson said was quite true. Over the years, Hoskins had succeeded in imprisoning many men who had opposed him, using trumped-up charges. The extent of the corrupt way in which he had wielded power in Warambe was only just beginning to come to light. The full realization of what would undoubtedly happen to him if he were to be thrown into prison among those men was written large in his eyes.

Letting out a sob, he suddenly launched himself at Yeoman, grabbing for the latter's holstered pistol. Yeoman sidestepped neatly, and Swalwell's outstretched foot brought Hoskins to grief, sending him sprawling on the floor with a crash.

Yeoman had had enough. He summoned two armed guards and indicated the grovelling Hoskins. 'Take him away and put him in the cooler,' he ordered. 'He can keep our American friend company for a while, until we make up our minds what we are going to do with the pair of them.' Hoskins, wailing protests, was dragged away.

'Wretched fellow,' Swalwell said. No further comment seemed necessary.

More reports were coming in from the river defences. With the spreading dawn, the action seemed to be dying away. In the key sectors, the Kerewatan forces appeared to be pulling back from the river. Those which had managed to cross over to the east bank under cover of darkness were now being heavily engaged by British units, fighting in the jungle, and quantities of prisoners were being taken.

As dawn broke over Kerewata, the Colonel brought his band of mercenary pilots to cockpit readiness. He was aware that something had gone wrong with Nkrombe's plan to destroy Warambe's uranium mines, for word of success should have reached the airfield HQ by now. Nevertheless, the planned withdrawal of the Kerewatan raiding forces was in full swing, and despite the fact that there had been no contact with Nkrombe since the previous evening he decided to go ahead and fly air cover over the river, more in the hope that the British might offer combat with their Hunters than out of any real desire to protect the Kerewatans.

He was the first to take off, accompanied by the two South Africans. Clouds hid the rising sun, so there was no fierce glare to contend with as they began their patrol along the river.

Below them, on the few roads that led from the river to the interior, Kerewatan troops straggled in a disorderly procession. Here and there, small craft dotted the river as raiding parties made their escape; the British appeared to be letting them go unmolested. The three Sabre pilots kept on scanning the eastern sky, but there was no sign of any opposition; the Hunters did not seem to be airborne. The Colonel wondered why. It was not like the British — and certainly not like their commanding officer, whom he knew of old — to sit on the ground when there was a prospect of action.

A second flight of Sabres arrived to take the place of the original three, which returned to base. Immediately after landing, the Colonel sought out Koppejans, whose mercenary troops were now solidly entrenched in defensive positions around the airfield perimeter.

'No sign of any trouble?' the Colonel asked. The Belgian shook his head.

'None. I've been sending out patrols some distance along the road into town, but they report no sign of Nkrombe's men. It's as though the whole Kerewatan army has gone to ground — apart from the fellows you saw retreating. There's been no word from my chaps at Nkrombe's residence either, which worries me. We heard a couple of bursts of machine-gun fire coming from the direction of the town sometime during the night, but that might not mean anything; maybe the Kerewatans were just getting drunk and letting off steam.'

'Maybe.' The Colonel remained unconvinced. 'I think that something is brewing,' he said. 'It's like the calm before the storm. All right — from now on there'll be no more patrols along the river. I'm keeping all my aircraft here, fuelled and armed, ready to take off instantly if we find ourselves with a fight on our hands.' He frowned, then said, 'There's something I don't understand. We both suspected that Nkrombe was about to unleash his forces against us. I'm beginning to think that we have done him an injustice. Maybe the Kerewatan army is about to turn on its master. If that is the case, I'm prepared to fight to save his neck, for one reason alone — he owes me a great deal of money, and I won't get it if he's dead.'

'I agree,' Koppejans said. 'I hate to think how my boys will react if I have to tell them that they won't be getting any wages because someone has strung up the boss.'

He paused and looked out across the airfield towards where his men held their positions. 'I ought to send a fighting group into Kerewata to find out exactly what is going on,' he said, 'but I don't want to deplete the defences here. Besides, my men would probably be ambushed.'

The Colonel had a brainwave. 'What we need is some air reconnaissance,' he stated. 'I'll take the Cessna, the one the South Africans brought with them. You can come along with me, if you like, or send one of your officers.'

'I'll come myself,' Koppejans told him. 'Anything's better than playing this waiting game. And two pairs of eyes are better than one, as the saying goes.'

They were airborne twenty minutes later, the Colonel having first issued orders that no more Sabre patrols were to be flown, but that the pilots were to remain at readiness to go into action if the airfield came under attack.

The Colonel stayed at low level, following the road that led from the airfield to Kerewata town. Within minutes the Cessna's occupants saw signs of movement by the roadside, several hundred feet beneath the little aircraft's wings. Koppejans pointed.

'There,' he shouted, 'trucks! And some armoured cars, too. They look to be stationary, but they are all pointed towards the airfield.'

The words were scarcely out of his mouth when tracers came snaking up towards the Cessna from machine-guns mounted on the turrets of the armoured vehicles. Hastily, the Colonel sheered off and circled the convoy at a safe distance.

'Well,' he commented grimly, 'at least we know who our enemies are.' He radioed the airfield, warning the men there to stand by for an impending attack, then resumed his course for Kerewata.

The streets of the provincial capital were deserted. The Colonel circled the town twice, then flew low over Nkrombe's residence. It was only then that he and Koppejans saw the bodies, sprawled in the courtyard.

Chapter Nine

THE SPECIAL FORCE'S MISSION TO CAPTURE NKROMBE would never be detailed in anything other than the most secret report. This is how it unfolded.

The first task of de Salis and his men, after crossing the river, was to commandeer some transport. It proved to be unexpectedly simple. Stealing like black shadows through the forest, they heard the sound of voices, and the sound brought them to a spot beside a road. On it stood a solitary truck, and beside it two Africans crouched, warming themselves at a small fire. They were laughing and joking with each other, and they passed into oblivion happily, with perhaps only a momentary flash of astonishment as they died.

De Salis' men hid the bodies carefully in the undergrowth, then piled into the truck as their commander slipped into the driver's seat and started the engine. They discovered that the vehicle carried crates of ammunition; its crew must have been on their way to the battle at the river when they decided to halt, either because they were not immediately needed or because they were afraid to go near the fighting that could be heard in the background. Either way, they had paid for their decision with their lives.

From his meticulous study of the available maps of Kerewata, de Salis knew that the road they were on led directly to the provincial capital. Turning the vehicle round, he set off through the night at a steady thirty miles per hour. The men in the back kept their weapons cocked and ready, and occasionally they thought they might have need of them, for they passed other trucks; however, the occupants of the latter, dim shapes in the gloom, only waved and shouted out what sounded like friendly greetings. There was never a suspicious challenge.

Not, at least, until they reached the town.

De Salis halted the vehicle briefly on the outskirts and glanced over his shoulder, through the hole in the flap at the rear of the cab.

'What's in those ammo boxes?' he asked into the darkened interior.

'Grenades, mostly,' was the reply. De Salis nodded in satisfaction. 'Good. Make sure you've got them handy. We might need to toss a few around on the way in.'

The truck rumbled slowly past the pitiful shanties that littered Kerewata's suburbs. It was still raining, which was to de Salis' advantage; they passed plenty of troops, but the latter were huddled around their fires with blankets over their heads, more interested in keeping dry and warm than in looking up to stare at the mud-spattered vehicle that lurched by.

Things began to change as the truck drew nearer the centre of the town. As the vehicle rounded a corner on the approach to the central square where Nkrombe's residence stood, its headlights picked out a barrier stretched across the road. The barrier, constructed from overturned carts, was manned by several African soldiers who crouched behind it as the truck crawled forward, only their heads and shoulders visible, weapons at the ready.

De Salis did not hesitate. 'I'm going through!' he yelled, and rammed his foot down on the accelerator pedal. As the vehicle shot forward, the NCO sitting next to de Salis in the cab leaned out of the window, machine-pistol in hand, and sprayed the road-block. Seconds later, the snub-nosed truck smashed into the middle of the barrier with a terrific jolt, hurling the carts aside in a welter of splintered wood. The Africans ran for their lives and were shot down in their tracks.

De Salis could see, now, the full extent of what was happening in the square in front of Nkrombe's residence, and for a moment was gripped by the sick awareness that he and his men might be too late.

The scene before him was straight out of the worst possible nightmare. The square was crowded with Nkrombe's African troops; it was impossible to count their numbers. Most of them seemed to be drunk, capering around the square with bottles in their hands, discharging firearms indiscriminately into the air. The noise was frightful; it was small wonder that no-one had noticed the truck's brutal passage through the road-block, nor heard the gunfire.

In the centre of the square four stakes had been erected. A man — a white man — was impaled upon each one, writhing and screaming in agony. De Salis knew at once that they must be the mercenaries who had been guarding Nkrombe. To add to their torment, fires had been lit at the base of each stake.

Sickened, de Salis turned to the NCO beside him. 'Shoot those four men as we go past,' he ordered. There was no need to issue any orders to the men in the back of the truck. They knew what to do.

De Salis headed flat out for the gates of the residence, on the other side of the square. Beside him, the NCO opened fire; the tortured bodies on the stakes jerked and went limp. From the back of the truck, the other men hurled grenades into the throng. Explosions cracked out in rapid succession and shrapnel sprayed across the square, scything down screaming men. De Salis drove straight through a group of Africans, who bounced off the truck like peas.

Behind the speeding truck, utter confusion reigned. The African troops, stupefied by drink, were milling around in terror, tripping over the bodies of their dead and dying comrades. The confusion was the Special Force's principal ally; it would give them time enough, perhaps, to carry out the task in hand.

The gates of the residence were wide open and unguarded. De Salis drove through and slewed the truck round, bringing it to a halt behind a wall where it would be sheltered from any gunfire.

The Special Force's drill was well rehearsed. Even before the vehicle halted, men were jumping down from the back and running over to the gateway, taking cover among the shadows and setting up light machine-guns to cover every approach across the square, which was now deserted except for its litter of sprawling bodies and the lifeless figures of the mercenaries, dangling on their burning stakes. Others disappeared into the darkness, their task to check out the exterior of the residence and to deal with sentries, if there were any.

De Salis, followed by five men, ran lightly up the steps that led to the main door of the residence and flattened himself against the jamb, flat on his belly. He thumbed back the hammers of his personal weapon, a sawn-off twelve-bore shotgun, and counted to three. Beside him, one of his men kicked open the door and another flung himself into the hall beyond, rolling over.

There were two African soldiers in the hall. One of them raised a pistol as the first Special Force man burst in, but he never had time to fire; a charge from de Salis' shotgun took him squarely in the chest, hurling him in bloody ruin against the wall. The second man was shot through the head by the Special Force commando who had kicked open the door and who now sprang into the hall.

De Salis rose and ran across the hall, followed by the others. Meticulously, they checked the rooms that led off it; all were empty except one, which contained the body of an African maidservant, sprawled across a table. She had been raped and shot.

'Upstairs,' de Salis ordered. A broad staircase led to the upper storey of the residence and they advanced up it cautiously, a few steps at a time, alert for every possible movement. They reached the landing, and almost fell over the body of Nkrombe's son, a boy of seventeen or so. His genitals had been hacked off and thrust into his mouth, and his staring eyes testified to the horror he had undergone before death gave him merciful release.

A few yards away lay the body of the boy's mother, the senior of Nkrombe's three wives. She lay on her back, her hands still clasped around the hilt of the knife that was thrust into her rib cage under her left breast. At least she had been spared the fate of the maidservant; de Salis hoped that she had also been spared the sight of her son's death agony.

At that moment, de Salis and his men stiffened as a muffled scream, accompanied by raucous laughter, came from behind a door at the far end of the landing. The scream tailed off to a whimper. De Salis injected another cartridge into the empty barrel of his shotgun and was beside the door in a few silent strides, his men flattened against the wall on either side.

De Salis dropped to one knee, his gun cradled in the crook of his right arm, and nodded to the man next to him. An instant later, the door crashed open.

There were five Kerewatan soldiers in the room, and they probably never knew what hit them. One of them, bending over the body of the man who was strapped to a bed by his wrists and ankles, half-turned just in time to see the man who killed him, outlined in the light of the electric bulb that dangled over the landing. De Salis blasted his head off his shoulders and then swung the gun towards a second man, hitting him low in the belly. He collapsed in a heap, screeching and clutching at himself, then coughed blood and was silent. The others were despatched equally as quickly.

De Salis walked forward into the blood-soaked room. The whimpering man on the bed, he saw at once, was Nkrombe. He was covered in small cuts; it looked as though his captors had been taking it in turns to torment him. 'Untie him,' de Salis ordered crisply. 'No time to clean him up now. And blindfold him.' Ruthless though he was, de Salis had no wish for Nkrombe to see what had happened to his wife and son.

Nkrombe, however, was too stupefied with shock and pain to care much about what was happening to him. Dumbly, he pulled on his trousers, which one of de Salis' men had retrieved from a corner of the room, and made no complaint when a strip of cloth was bound over his eyes. He spoke only once, asking in a trembling voice who his rescuers were.

'Never mind about that,' de Salis told him. 'We've come to get you out of here. Let's go.'

Nkrombe did not enquire about the fate of his family. He must already have guessed, perhaps had even seen, what had become of them.

The residence echoed suddenly to the chatter of machine-gun fire. There was no time to lose. Quickly, de Salis and his men bundled Nkrombe out of the room and down the stairs, past the pitiful bodies of the woman and boy. A Special Force soldier reported to de Salis as they reached the main doorway.

'The surrounds are clear, sir,' he said. 'The exit at the rear, which was shown on our map of the residence, had been sealed off, but we've blown it. It's big enough for the truck to get through. The road on the other side leads through the north-west outskirts.'

'Right.' De Salis gave Nkrombe a shove. 'Get him into the truck and keep his head down. You others — ' he turned to the men who had helped him rescue Nkrombe '— you others join the chaps at the gate and lay down as much covering fire as you can. The moment I give the word, into the truck as fast as you can. I won't be hanging around.'

The shooting from across the square was sporadic, but growing in intensity all the time. The Special Force men were replying to it with short, accurate bursts, conserving their ammunition. There was no immediate danger that they might be overwhelmed by a suicidal charge.

De Salis started the truck, still in the shelter of the wall, and turned it so that its bonnet was pointing into the darkness at the rear of the residence. Leaning out of the cab, he gestured at the men defending the gateway. At once, they began to fall back towards him in a well-rehearsed movement, two at a time. As the last of them piled into the vehicle, their comrades hurled a shower of grenades over the wall into the square to deter any sudden move by the Africans, for a few seconds at least.

With everyone safely on board, de Salis sent the truck lurching away across the residence gardens towards the rear entrance. A minute later they were through and away, speeding along the narrow road out of town with headlights full on, unmindful of anything now except speed. Beside de Salis, the NCO was peering at a map by the light of a small torch.

'How far?' de Salis yelled, swinging the wheel to negotiate a sudden bend.

'About fifteen miles,' the NCO answered, his finger tracing their route. 'There's a junction just outside the town. Turn left there, and the road heads straight into the forest and doubles back on itself for a while. It peters out near a village, but then there's a track leading south. It'll be tough going, but at least it'll be taking us in the right direction, and it'll be better than walking. It runs through secondary forest, so we'll have some cover. After that, it looks as though we'll have to strike out across country. If everything goes well, we should reach our destination shortly before dawn.' He grinned suddenly, his teeth white in the darkness. 'I expect that's when our troubles really start,' he commented.

De Salis grinned back. 'Let's cross our bridges as we come to them,' he said. 'At least we've got this far.'

The NCO'S map, based on one obligingly supplied by a Belgian intelligence organization, was surprisingly accurate. As the NCO had predicted, the main track ended at a native village and became a muddy footpath, veering away to the south. De Salis nosed his way cautiously along it, the wheels of the truck crunching through the undergrowth on either side. Once, turning to avoid a large tree, he lost sight of it altogether, and was forced to stop while the NCO got down and cast about him with the beam of his torch. It was five minutes before he found the path again and guided the truck back on to it.

Several times, the vehicle got bogged down in marshy patches and had to be pushed clear by the occupants, who had jettisoned most of its load of ammunition *en route*, keeping only a few boxes of grenades and 7.62-mm rounds.

At last, after a couple of hours of crawling through the forest, de Salis, his eyes bloodshot with the effort of peering through the darkness, brought the truck to a stop with a suddenness that brought some grunts of protest from the men in the back. There was no track ahead any more; just a large expanse of swamp. The headlights picked out grassy tufts, spaced at regular intervals, that might have provided firm footholds for a man, but de Salis knew that this was as far as he could take the vehicle.

'Now what?' he asked the NCO.

'It's all right, sir,' the man replied cheerfully. 'The swamp is marked on the map, right here. From now on, we're on foot. We skirt the edge of it until we come to a rise in the ground, then we take a compass bearing of 030 magnetic. A two-mile march through the forest, and we're there.'

'Let's get on with it, then,' de Salis ordered. 'Everybody out. Bring some grenades, but leave the rest. How's Nkrombe?'

'Seems to have come round a bit, sir,' one of the men answered. 'We've cleaned up his cuts. He'll be okay.'

De Salis stayed in the truck as the others got down. There was one more thing he felt he had to do. With everyone safely out, he engaged first gear, released the handbrake and then jumped clear himself. The truck lunged forward and nosed into the mud with a gurgling sound. In time, the swamp would swallow it completely.

The NCO looked at de Salis enquiringly. 'Well,' the latter said rather lamely, 'she's served us pretty well. Doesn't seem right for the locals to pull her to bits for scrap, somehow.'

They set off on a compass bearing through the forest, taking it in turns to half-carry the corpulent Nkrombe. It was an exhausting march, for the near-impenetrable darkness made it hard to see obstacles in their path. Fortunately, only light undergrowth lay across their track and they were never compelled to hack their way.

Apart from their laboured breathing, they marched in silence for an hour and a half. Light was beginning to filter through the trees, making progress a little easier. Suddenly, at the head of the column, de Salis raised his hand. They halted and stood like statues, listening.

From somewhere up ahead, a deep rumble split the silence. It grew in volume, resolving itself into the unmistakable shriek of jet engines, then died away. De Salis took a deep breath of relief.

'All right, boys,' he said, 'not far now. Come on.'

They set off again with renewed vigour. De Salis fell back a little and hooked one of Nkrombe's arms around his neck, grunting at the sudden burden of the exhausted man.

'Where are you taking me?' the African croaked, speaking for the first time since the march began.

'Don't worry,' de Salis told him, 'we're getting you out. Hold on. It won't be long.' He spoke with an assurance he did not feel.

After another half hour's march, the forest began to thin out. They went ahead more cautiously now, as the spreading dawn began to show through the screen of trees that marked the forest's limit.

Beyond the forest lay Kerewata airstrip, the boundary of which was separated from the forest by a fifty-yard stretch of open ground. Accompanied by several of his men, de Salis crept forward and surveyed the area. There did not appear to be any defences on this side of the field, and de Salis reasoned that any defenders must be concentrated on the north-east sector, where any threat would be most likely to develop.

'What now, sir?' whispered the NCO who had map-read their way to the airfield.

'We wait,' de Salis answered. 'We wait, and we watch.'

A few minutes later, three Sabres came whistling in from the south-east, dropping into line astern over the airfield and landing behind one another. De Salis watched as they taxied over to the far side of the airfield and vanished from sight. The minutes ticked by slowly, then the NCO tapped de Salis' arm, pointing. A light twin-engined aircraft, painted blue and white, was taxiing out towards the end of the runway. It took off with a throaty roar of engines and headed northwards at low altitude, towards Kerewata town.

De Salis looked at his watch. It was 0530. 'H-hour is set for 0630,' he muttered, half to himself. He turned to the NCO. 'Better break out some rations,' he said. 'It might be some time before we eat again.'

They munched their cold breakfast, and continued their vigil. After a while, the light aircraft returned and landed, parking near the control tower on the other side of the field. It was now 0610.

De Salis slid back through the undergrowth and spoke to three of his men, each of whom carried a bulky pack. 'Is everything okay?' he asked.

The senior of the men nodded. 'Yes, sir. The equipment checks out okay. We can have it up in about five minutes, maybe less.'

'Good. We won't have much time.' He looked out across the airfield, narrowing his eyes against the glare of the rising sun. The dark silhouettes of three more Sabres emerged from it; like the first three, they broke into line astern and landed, the wail of their turbojets dying away.

I hope Yeoman and Sampson have done their job, de Salis told himself, or we're done for. It was now fifteen minutes to H-hour. Ten more minutes, and they would have to make their move.

Chapter Ten

YEOMAN SAT IN THE COCKPIT OF HIS HUNTER, ENGINE idling, ready for take-off. The other seven Hunters were behind him, their pilots eager for the prospect of some action.

The vast bulk of the Beverley transport aircraft was little more than a dot on the western horizon; they would catch up with it over the river and then pass it, ready to deal with any opposition.

He ran over the details of the operation in his mind, smiling to himself as he did so; Sampson, as usual, had preserved secrecy right up to the last minute, but now Yeoman knew why a heavy guard had been placed on the Beverley, and why no-one had been allowed near it. If unauthorized eyes had spotted the equipment inside it, the game might have been given away.

Sampson had insisted on flying aboard the transport aircraft to supervise the operation personally. Considerable danger was involved, for the mercenary pilots, unaware of what was happening, would almost certainly try to intercept it. Determined attempts had been made throughout the night by Sampson's signals people to contact the mercenary HQ at Kerewata, but to no avail. It was the one flaw in an otherwise impeccable plan. If the mercenaries could have been contacted, they might have been persuaded not to take action against the British; as it was, no-one quite knew what would happen.

Yeoman was convinced that they would try to shoot down the Beverley, perhaps in the belief that it contained paratroops. The job of his Hunter pilots was to stop them.

It was time. Yeoman pressed the R/T button.

'Red Section, take off.'

He opened the throttle and the Hunter began to roll as a surge of power went through its Rolls-Royce Avon engine. The jet fighter accelerated rapidly, and Yeoman felt the rudder begin to 'bite' as the airspeed indicator showed 90 knots. At 120 knots, a slight backward pressure on the stick raised the nosewheel off the ground, and at 150 knots the aircraft flew itself into the air.

Yeoman tucked up his undercarriage and went into a left-hand orbit of the field, allowing the others to catch up with him. Then, in battle formation, they climbed away at a steady 430 knots, following the path of the Beverley.

They levelled out at eight thousand feet and quickly overhauled the lumbering transport. It looked weird and box-like, for the clamshell doors at the rear of its cargo hold had been removed. Yeoman glanced back: the four Hunters of yellow section were half a mile to the rear and above, in finger-four formation.

He pressed the R/T button again. There was no need to maintain radio silence. 'Hunter squadron, keep your eyes peeled. Yellow section, maintain altitude. Red section, descend to four thousand feet.'

Yeoman's four aircraft went into a shallow dive, levelling out as though held together by a thread. Their objective, Kerewata airfield, was five minutes' flying time away. Every instinct told him to take all eight Hunters down in a blazing attack on the objective, destroying the mercenaries' Sabres before they could get airborne, but such were not his orders. His brief was to protect the Beverley, and to defend himself only if attacked first. To him, the orders seemed utterly illogical, but he supposed there must be some political reasoning behind them. Maybe, he thought, they might be lucky enough to complete the operation without risk; maybe the mercenary pilots were having breakfast.

*

They were not. As soon as the Colonel had landed, having assessed the situation in Kerewata and reasoned that the airfield might soon come under attack by rebel forces, he brought his pilots to cockpit readiness. Six Sabres, including his own, were combat-ready; three more, the last to return from patrol, were hurriedly being refuelled and rearmed.

The Colonel radioed the control tower, from where Koppejans was supervising the defences, and asked if anything was happening. The controller handed the microphone to the Belgian.

'Not a thing, as yet,' Koppejans said. 'The Africans are making no move, although one of my reconnaissance patrols reports that they have been joined by more units who have pulled back from the river. I think ... hold on a second.'

The Belgian had been interrupted by the controller, who had been scanning the eastern sky through powerful binoculars merely for the sake of something to do. He gave a gasp of astonishment when several black dots swam into his field of vision. Adjusting the focus slightly, he handed the glasses to Koppejans. 'What do you make of that?' he asked.

Koppejans looked, and did not need to look again. Grabbing the microphone, he yelled: 'Get airborne! There are planes coming in from the direction of Warambe. They'll be here in minutes!'

'Let's go,' the Colonel said over the radio, and waved to his ground crew. The starter cartridge ignited with a thump and soon the Sabre's engine was fully lit, its shrill whine rising sharply as the rpm climbed. Soon, all six aircraft were moving, taxiing out towards the end of the strip as fast as it was safe to go, the pilots carrying out their cockpit checks as they went.

The Colonel was the first to take off, followed closely by Jan and Piet, who over the past few days he had come to recognize as by far the most skilful of his band of pilots. Whipping up their undercarriages, they went into a hard climbing turn to the right, intending to face the threat coming in from the east.

They were fractionally too late. Even as they turned, four Hunters blasted low across the airfield in a thunderclap of sound, pulling thin trails of black smoke. The British fighters pulled up steeply and broke to left and right, gaining several thousand feet of altitude. Four more jets crossed the field at a higher level.

The Colonel and his two wingmen went on turning, keeping pace with the nearest pair of Hunters. Below them, the other three Sabres were taking off, one after the other. The Colonel was puzzled. If the British had wanted to, they could easily have destroyed the three Sabres on the ground, and then turned on the three that were already in the air, but they were making no move to attack.

He ordered his pilots to continue climbing and to keep a watchful eye on the British jets. He would wait for the Hunters to make the first move. Soon, the last three Sabres would also be airborne, and then he would have a numerical advantage.

He glanced down to see what was happening on the airstrip, and immediately caught sight of something very odd. In the extreme south-east corner of the field, a bright orange-coloured object was rising slowly into the air. Quickly, he radioed Koppejans and told the Belgian what he had seen. Koppejans came on the air after a few seconds' delay.

'Looks like a balloon of some sort,' he said. 'Can't quite make out what's going on. I'll send some of my chaps to investigate.'

The time was just after 0630 hours. Five minutes earlier, Peter de Salis and his men, unobserved by anyone, had quietly crept forward from their place of concealment at the edge of the forest into a patch of open ground on the airfield itself. While some of the Special Force men fanned out and assumed defensive positions, others busied themselves with the bulky packs that they had brought with them. As they did so, the first flight of Sabres thundered into the air, and almost immediately afterwards the Hunters swept across the field.

De Salis glanced up at the jets, circling watchfully around each other, and nodded with satisfaction. So far, the plan seemed to be working.

The mysterious packs were quickly opened and their contents laid out on the ground. First came a roll of orange material which, when spread out, resolved itself into the deflated envelope of a balloon. A small gas cylinder was attached to its neck. Next came a harness and a hundred-foot length of super-tough nylon rope. One end was clipped to a fitting on the balloon envelope, the other to the harness. A few feet from the balloon, the rope passed through a curious cross-shaped metal structure, which was held in place by strong clips. The metal was titanium, one of the strongest and lightest alloys devised by man.

'Get him into the harness,' de Salis ordered, indicating Nkrombe. Within seconds, the African was trussed up like a turkey in what was really a modified parachute harness. He sat cross-legged on the ground, arms folded across his chest, dumbly wondering what strange fate awaited him.

'Here she comes, sir,' one of the Special Force men said, pointing. 'Right on time.'

De Salis looked. Low over the forest, still a couple of miles distant, the great bulk of the Beverley cruised slowly towards the airfield.

'Inflate,' de Salis ordered. One of his men turned a valve, and helium gas hissed from the cylinder into the envelope of the balloon. It writhed like a crushed slug, then began to billow out as the gas filled it. In thirty seconds it was rising from the ground, trailing its length of rope. Below the neck of the balloon, the metal cross revolved slowly, glinting in the sunlight which was now beginning to penetrate the eastern cloud bank.

On the flight deck of the Beverley, Air Commodore Sampson, in the co-pilot's seat, peered ahead and saw the tiny disc of the balloon as it rose against the backdrop of the forest on the far side of the airfield. The pilot had seen it too, although he was preoccupied with the activities of the jet fighters circling over the field. He moved the control column and the huge aircraft responded ponderously.

'I'm going to make my run from the south,' he said over the intercom, 'straight into wind. That'll reduce our ground speed and increase our chances of a first-time hook-up.'

Sampson looked at him and nodded. 'Roger.' He spoke over the intercom to the men standing by in the Beverley's great, barn-like cargo hold. 'Extend your gear,' he told them.

A few moments later, a strange, trapeze-like structure emerged over the lip of the cargo hold and swung down into the slipstream, held rigidly in place by two metal arms. 'Gear in position, sir,' one of the operators told the men on the flight deck.

As the Beverley turned, Sampson looked out of the side window. He was in time to see two Sabres, a few thousand feet higher up, curving round in what looked like the start of an attack pattern. He said nothing to the pilot; there was no point. Either the Hunters would do their work, or the Beverley would end up as a sixty-ton pile of blazing scrap metal.

Up above, Yeoman spotted the sudden move made by the Sabres, the last ones to take off, and swore to himself. Their aggressive intentions made it plain that no contact had been established with the mercenaries, as he had hoped. He snapped an order over the R/T.

'Yellow Section, two bandits heading for the transport, diving from one o'clock.'

The warning was unnecessary; Bright, leading Yellow Section, had already spotted the danger and was bringing his four Hunters down to head off the Sabres. The pilots of the latter, both Frenchmen, saw the Hunters coming down on them and one of them turned towards the British jets, leaving the other to continue his attack on the Beverley. Bright, covered by his wingman, went after this aircraft. The Hunter was much faster than the American fighter and overhauled it rapidly. Bright closed in to four hundred yards' range and fired a burst with his cannon, seeing the flash of a shell burst on the Sabre's dark green fuselage, aft of the cockpit. The Sabre at once pulled up sharply, losing speed and presenting a plan-view target to the RAF pilot, who fired a second burst from one hundred yards. This time, pieces flew off the Sabre as Bright's shells found their mark on its port wing. There was a puff of smoke which rapidly turned into a sheet of flame as the Sabre came apart in a blaze of exploding fuel tanks. The fragments described a long parabola through the air and impacted on the eastern edge of the airfield.

The second Sabre pilot pulled back the stick and climbed hard, zooming up almost vertically. One of the Hunter pilots, Yellow Four, went after it. Bright ordered him to break off the engagement and rejoin the others, but the Hunter pilot, who was Peter Gibbons, did not appear to have heard the instruction. He continued his climb, intent on achieving what would have been his first 'kill'.

High above, Yeoman's four Hunters and the Colonel's three Sabres were still circling the airfield cautiously, sizing one another up like packs of dogs about to launch themselves into a fight. The Colonel was beside himself with fury, for the two Frenchmen had begun their attack on the transport without his authority, and now one of them had paid with his life. The second would soon do so, too, unless prompt action saved him.

The Colonel pressed the R/T button and called his wingmen, telling them to cover him, and then winged over in a dive towards the two climbing jets. Passing the Frenchman's Sabre in a blur of speed, he attacked Gibbons' Hunter head-on, firing one short burst before he was forced to pull out of his dive as the ground rushed up to meet him. His bullets struck the Hunter on its starboard air intake and removed several feet of metal skin from the wing root. Startled, his mind overtaken by the speed of the sudden attack, Gibbons rolled out of the climb and brought his damaged aircraft into level flight. More metal fragments whirled away in the slipstream. Before he had time to think, the Avon engine flamed out and the Hunter began to descend in a glide towards the airfield below. Frantically, he tried to relight the engine as the altimeter unwound with sickening speed, but the Avon remained dead. At last, down to five hundred feet, he pulled the face-blind handle of his ejection seat and blasted himself out of the cockpit.

Meanwhile, the Beverley, as yet unmolested, was turning back towards the airfield from the south. De Salis watched it coming in, so low that its stalky fixed undercarriage almost brushed the ground. He warned Nkrombe to brace himself, then glanced across the airfield; a small armoured scout car, still a long way off, was racing towards his group. Quickly, he turned to his NCO.

'Tell the men to fall back to the edge of the forest,' he ordered. 'We'll be in trouble if that scout car catches us out in the open.'

There might just be time enough, he thought, as he turned his attention back to the approaching Beverley. If, that is, the pilot gets it right first time.

In the Beverley's cockpit, Sampson found himself holding his breath as the pilot held a rock-steady course towards the orange balloon. Above the airfield, a battle seemed to be developing as the Hunter pilots tangled with the Sabres, preventing the latter from interfering with the transport aircraft.

The roar of the Beverley's four Bristol Centaurus engines became deafening as the huge aircraft thundered closer, its trapeze fully extended. Its belly brushed the orange balloon, and a moment later there was an audible slap as the trapeze struck the nylon rope. The metal bar of the trapeze slid rapidly up the rope and struck the cross-piece just below the balloon, tripping a device that caused the four arms of the metal cross to fold inwards and lock firmly into position around the bar.

The rope snapped taut and Nkrombe gave an involuntary cry as his harness bit into him. Instantly, he was whipped off the ground, a grotesque figure, trailing behind the Beverley, his arms and legs flailing in terror. In the belly of the aircraft, the crew set about the task of reeling him in. The pilot climbed a little, in order to clear the trees, and turned away from the airfield. Up above, Yeoman heard his radio call, saying that the pickup run had been successful.

Yeoman had his hands full. His task, and that of his pilots, was to shepherd the Beverley safely home, but the Sabre pilots were showing more signs of fight than he had anticipated. They flew aggressively and with discipline, making it impossible for the British pilots to break off the action cleanly.

A quick glance told him that the Beverley was turning away to the south of the airfield, levelling out with its nose pointing eastwards, in the direction of Warambe. He ordered his section to edge their way towards the transport while the three remaining Hunters of Yellow Section kept the Sabres busy. The mercenary squadron had now lost another aircraft; flown by one of the Germans, the Sabre had fallen victim to Flight

Lieutenant Neil Hart, who had nailed it with a single short burst from five hundred yards. The Sabre had banked steeply to the left and had then turned into the ground, exploding in a huge sheet of flame among the trees to the east of the field. The pilot had not got out.

The two sides were evenly matched now, in terms of numbers; it was seven against seven. Yeoman looked up and to the rear. A section of three Sabres was turning towards the lumbering Beverley, and a fourth — possibly the aircraft that had shot down Gibbons — was climbing to join them. Rapping a curt order over the R/T, Yeoman led his four Hunters on a course that would intercept the hostile formation.

Meanwhile, their mission accomplished, de Salis and his men had once again taken cover in the forest, seconds before the scout car sped on to the scene. The armoured vehicle's machine-gun sprayed the trees, sending a spatter of wood splinters flying in all directions. The scout car drew off a little and sat there, squat and menacing, its machine-gun moving from side to side in search of a target. De Salis ordered his men to lie low and wait to see what happened. If contact had been established with the mercenaries, they might find themselves with some unexpected allies. If not, they were likely to be caught in the middle of a battle between the mercenaries and the Kerewatan troops. In either event, they would have to fight their way out.

Through the screen of trees, they could see something of the air battle that had developed overhead. The Beverley was well on its way by now, its bulk dwindling in the distance. Two groups of aircraft were chasing after it, one composed of Sabres, the other of Hunters.

Yeoman, in the leading Hunter of Red Section, curved in pursuit of the foremost Sabre, whose pilot seemed intent on catching the retreating Beverley and shooting it down at all costs. The other three Sabres suddenly broke hard to the left, climbing and turning steeply, which was their mistake; the manoeuvre placed them in loose line astern, which meant that they stayed right in front of the pursuing Hunters. Two of the Hunters immediately broke hard after them and Yeoman ordered his wingman to join them, feeling confident that he could deal with the lone Sabre out in front.

In level flight the Hunter had a far better acceleration than the American fighter, and Yeoman saw with relief that he would be well within range long before the Sabre managed to overtake the Beverley.

The Sabre pilot knew it, too, and suddenly racked his fighter round in a maximum-rate turn to the right. Yeoman followed him, his body suddenly five times its normal weight as the 'g' force gripped him.

The Sabre pilot was going to fight on the turn, and the reasoning behind his choice was simple. Because of its better thrust-weight ratio, the Hunter was faster then the Sabre in level flight and the climb. It was also very manoeuvrable at low speed, but in a turn the British fighter's drag curve rose sharply and its extra thrust could not compensate for this. The overall result was that speed in a turn tended to fall off quite dramatically. It was obvious that the Sabre pilot wanted to put Yeoman into this position; if he could get on the Hunter's tail, Yeoman would not be able to out-turn him. The Sabre pilot could then catch up with the Hunter, tightening up his own turn at fairly low speed in order to get inside his opponent's turning radius, and then open fire.

Yeoman, an old hand at this sort of game, had no intention of allowing any such thing to happen. Reducing his speed, he lowered the Hunter's nose and then flicked the fighter into a low-speed 'yo-yo', rolling over and pulling over to cut inside the Sabre's turn. The manoeuvre, devised by fighter pilots during the Second World War, was designed to bring the pursuing fighter gradually closer to his opponent's six o'clock position and break the stalemate of a turning fight.

For a moment, as he rolled out of the 'yo-yo' and the luminous pipper of his gunsight crept towards the Sabre's tail pipe, Yeoman thought that the manoeuvre had worked, and almost immediately realized that it had not. His speed was still a good deal higher than the Sabre's, and the mercenary pilot, whoever he was, took full advantage of the fact.

As Yeoman closed in, intent on achieving a kill, the Sabre suddenly pulled up into a high-g barrel roll, a manoeuvre designed to turn the tables on an opponent approaching with excess speed. It was a dangerous form of defence, because the aircraft carrying it out lost a great deal of speed, and if the pilot's timing was not exactly right he ended up dead. If he pulled into the roll too late, the pursuing fighter would swat him like a fly as he hung defencelessly in mid-roll, with no manoeuvring capability; if he began the roll too soon, the attacker would see it coming, zoom-climb for height and then dive down to complete his kill.

The Sabre pilot got it exactly right, as Yeoman found to his cost a moment later. Unable to manoeuvre crisply because of his high speed, he shot through the middle of his opponent's roll, like a thread passing through the eye of a needle. Breaking hard, he frantically searched the sky to the rear of the cockpit, and was just in time to see the Sabre arcing round on to his tail as it came out of its roll.

It was time to think fast. Yeoman knew that he had met his match in terms of skill and experience. He had to pull something out of the hat, quickly, or his twenty years as a fighter pilot would come to an abrupt end in this stinking backwater. As his mind raced, the Sabre pilot opened fire.

The battle had taken the two jets well to the east of the airfield, over the jungle. From the field itself, three tall columns of smoke rose into the morning air, two from the shattered wrecks of Sabres, the third from Peter Gibbons' Hunter, which had struck the ground at a shallow angle and had bounced across the airfield for two hundred yards before exploding.

Gibbons, exiting at low level from his crashing fighter, had landed near the control tower with a thump that broke one of his ankles and momentarily knocked him unconscious.

When he came to, it was to find himself lying on his back with three men bending over him. Automatically, he groped for his parachute's quick-release box, but someone had already stripped him of his harness.

The men bending over him were white, their faces bronzed by the African sun, and they wore jungle-green fatigues. One of them had some kind of silver insignia on his epaulettes. Gibbons, badly shaken, struggled to sit up and addressed him, asking if he spoke English. The other nodded.

'I want to see your commander,' Gibbons said. 'It's urgent. There's an important message.'

'I am the commander,' Koppejans told him. 'What is it you want?'

Gibbons shivered slightly as reaction began to set in. He swallowed with difficulty.

'Our people have been trying to make contact with you,' he said. 'The Kerewatan Army is in revolt.'

'I know that,' Koppejans said. 'But go on.'

'We've got Nkrombe. That was what the transport aircraft was for. We tried to warn you not to resist, but for some reason our people haven't been able to get through. Can't you call off your pilots?'

'They are not my pilots,' Koppejans pointed out. 'And anyway, why should I trust you?'

Helplessly, Gibbons gestured towards the rising columns of smoke. 'Your men are dying needlessly,' he said, gasping as a spasm of pain from his shattered ankle shot through him. 'Call them off. Tell them to divert to Warambe. You are going to have to fight your way out of here, and you'll need all the air cover you can get. There's a plan to let your pilots operate alongside our own,' he lied.

Koppejans straightened up. 'Very well,' he said. 'I will send out the necessary instructions. Meanwhile, we had better get you under cover.'

At that moment, as if to underline the truth of what Gibbons had just said, three artillery shells burst on the airfield. From the perimeter defences, close to the main gate, a heavy machine-gun hammered. At last, the rebel Kerewatan forces had decided to make their move.

A very few minutes later, the mercenary pilots who were still engaging the Hunters, with no further losses on either side thanks to the high skill of the opposing forces, were surprised to hear Koppejans' voice suddenly burst over the R/T. The mercenary commander identified himself in plain language.

'This is Koppejans. The airfield is under attack. Do not land. I repeat, the airfield is under attack. Do not land. Divert to Warambe. Acknowledge your instructions.'

One by one, the surviving Sabre pilots complied, breaking off their sparring with the Hunters and withdrawing to the west of the field to form up. In loose formation, they circled slowly round the perimeter and set course for the river. The pilots were puzzled by the sudden turn of events, but below them they could see shells bursting on the solitary runway and knew that any attempt to land would be suicidal. Short of baling out into heaven knew what, Warambe was their only alternative.

On the far side of the airfield, Peter de Salis, still under cover at the edge of the forest and menaced by the scout car, also experienced a shock of surprise when, through the screen of undergrowth, he saw the hatch in the armoured vehicle's squat turret open and a hand emerge, waving what looked like a white handkerchief. He hissed an order to his men, telling them to hold their fire.

A moment later, cautiously, the hand was followed by a head and shoulders and a voice rang out, speaking in what might have been an Australian accent.

'Hey, you blokes. We've just had a radio signal. Looks as though we're on the same side all of a sudden. Can I talk to your boss?'

After a moment's hesitation, de Salis yelled, 'All right! But come down out of there, where I can see you. And no tricks.' He rose slowly to his feet and ordered his men, 'Keep me covered.'

The scout car commander climbed down and came forward. The two men stood face to face on the edge of the forest, and de Salis noted that the mercenary's bearded face wore an expression of bewilderment.

'This is a funny business,' he said. 'I've just had orders to rejoin the main force and invite you to come along. The airfield is under attack,' he added, stating the obvious. 'Anyway, who the hell are you?'

'Never mind about that,' de Salis told him firmly. 'All you need to know is that your former boss, Nkrombe, is on his way to Warambe, and I suggest we all start heading in that direction as soon as possible. It's going to get very unhealthy around here. With our firepower added to yours, we might just about make it.'

High above the airfield, the Hunters turned towards the Sabre formation, ready to attack. But the Sabres were showing no aggressive intentions; they were flying very slowly, and as the RAF pilots watched, the leading Sabre lowered its undercarriage in a gesture of surrender.

Norman Bright, who had vainly been trying to contact Yeoman over the R/T, assumed command.

'They're heading for Warambe,' he told the other pilots. 'The message must have got through to them. Stay above and astern; if they change their minds and decide to fight again, we'll hit them hard.' He paused, and then asked, 'Has anybody seen any sign of Red Leader?'

None of them had. Then Neil Hart, flying on the extreme left of the Hunter formation, drew Bright's attention to something ahead.

Bright looked, and felt his heart sink. From the jungle, close to the road that led to the main river crossing, two oily mushrooms of smoke rose slowly above the treetops. Bright knew, from long experience, that at the base of those sinister clouds lay the burning wreckage of aircraft.

Chapter Eleven

YEOMAN PULLED HARD RIGHT IN AN ATTEMPT TO EVADE the stream of machine-gun bullets that lanced towards him, and knew at once that he was too late. The Hunter shuddered as the bullets struck it somewhere aft of the cockpit. He kept on turning, pressure-induced contrails streaming from his wing-tips, and felt another burst of fire strike home.

The Sabre was very close astern, its nose lit by the flashes of its gunfire. Behind him, Yeoman sensed rather than heard a terrific bang and his seat harness bit into him suddenly as the Hunter decelerated. At the same moment, the control column went sloppy in his hand and the fighter began to roll to the left.

He reached down and grabbed the seat-pan handle, saving a vital fraction of a second. An instant later, with a jolt that compressed him from neck to buttocks, the Martin-Baker seat kicked him out into space.

Less than a hundred yards astern of the Hunter, the Colonel watched the smoke trails of his bullets punch into the British fighter's fuselage and felt a surge of elation. He fired again, saw white fuel vapour stream behind his target, and saw the Hunter waver. Its left wing started to drop. Then its glittering cockpit canopy flew off and the dark bundle of ejection seat and pilot punched out in a puff of grey smoke.

Before the Colonel even had time to think about turning away from his kill, the Hunter exploded. It tumbled on across the tree tops, trailing streamers of blazing fuel and scattering debris in all directions. Instinctively, the Colonel raised an arm over his face as his Sabre's speed took him straight through the heart of the inferno.

A series of dull thuds shook the fighter as its gaping air intake ingested lethal fragments of metal. The pilot hauled back the stick and the Sabre reared up, vibrating horribly. Behind the cockpit, unseen, a turbine disc came adrift and ripped through the side of the fuselage, biting great chunks out of the port wing before it whirled away.

Time froze as the Colonel reached down and, as though in slow motion, grasped the ejection seat handle, built into the arm-rest of his seat. Then, as the Sabre reached the top of its climb, breaking up as it went, he too blasted out of the cockpit.

Unlike the Hunter, the Sabre was not fitted with a fully-automatic seat. Desperately, for he knew that his life was measured in seconds, the Colonel twisted the mechanism of the seat-harness release and kicked himself free, at the same time pulling the D-ring of his parachute. For what seemed an age, he and the seat went on falling together; then a ribbon of silk streamed from his parachute pack as the drogue deployed, slowing him down, and the seat dropped away beneath him.

The small drogue pulled the main parachute canopy clear and it deployed over his head with a crack and a jerk that sent the breath gasping out of his body.

There was neither the time, nor the height, for him to worry about searching for a clear patch among the trees that were now rapidly rushing up to meet him. He held his legs tightly together and crossed his arms over his face to protect his eyes as he plummeted into the forest canopy at a slight angle. Branches whipped at him and something caught him a painful blow on the shoulder. Then there came another fearsome jerk and his downward progress was halted abruptly. He swung backwards like a pendulum and struck a tree trunk with a bruising force that knocked the wind out of him a second time. His arms dropped limply to his sides as he hung there, stunned and unable to move, his parachute canopy caught fast in the branches of the tree that had broken his fall.

Regaining his senses, he opened his eyes and saw immediately that he was suspended less than six feet from the jungle floor. He moved his legs in an effort to find out whether anything was broken; it did not seem to be, so he took a chance and banged the quick-release box of his parachute harness. A moment later, he was sprawling on the spongy ground at the base of the tree, his first sensation one of relief at being free from the biting constraint of his parachute straps.

He stood up, trying to get his bearings. Through the trees, some distance away, he saw a bright glow and heard the roar of a fierce fire; the noise was accompanied by the sharp crack of exploding ammunition.

He glanced up at the sunlight that filtered through the trees and worked out that the main Kerewata-Warambe road lay on his left, in the direction of the fire. He began to walk towards it, and in a few minutes came upon a scene of devastation.

The crashing Hunter, his recent victim, had torn a great swathe through the trees, scattering metal fragments everywhere. One of its wings was impaled on a splintered trunk; there was no sign of the other, or of the tail. The engine lay smouldering and crumpled among the undergrowth, while the fuselage, blazing fiercely, had been reduced to a pile of twisted scrap metal.

The Colonel was used to the sight of the shattered remnants of aircraft. What caught his attention now was the parachute canopy, almost entirely consumed by the flames, that lay close to the broken fuselage. Some distance away, still attached to the canopy by his harness and shroud lines, a man lay face-down in the mud, motionless.

At first the Colonel thought he was dead, but then he saw the man's right arm twitch feebly. Braving the intense heat, the mercenary pilot ran across to the sprawled figure and turned it over. He twisted the round metal quick-release box of the parachute harness and struck it a sharp blow, causing the harness to fall apart. Then, gripping the man under the armpits, he dragged him away from the encroaching flames.

A rapid inspection told him that the pilot did not seem to be badly hurt. There was a nasty bruise on the side of his face and a cut on the eyebrow above it, but no bones appeared to be broken. He unfastened the man's flying helmet and tossed it aside into the undergrowth.

He looked down at the face of the unconscious pilot, and at once knew the identity of the man he had shot down. He knew, also, what he had to do.

Suddenly, he raised his head, listening. Over the crackle of the flames, he caught the sound of a truck's engine. The road must not be far away. There was no way of telling who was in the truck, and he did not propose to take any chances. Using a fireman's lift, he hoisted the dead weight of the other pilot and stumbled away among the trees until he came upon a tangle of undergrowth. He lowered the other carefully to the ground and then lay down beside him, peering back towards the wreck of the Hunter.

After a while, several men emerged from the forest on the far side of the wreck and approached it cautiously. The Colonel saw that they were Kerewatan troops. He watched as they circled the debris, prodding at bits of wreckage with their rifles. Then one of them spotted the parachute harness, and called out excitedly to the others. He bent over, peering at the ground, and the Colonel knew that he must have seen footprints in the mud. The man stood upright and shouted, pointing vaguely towards the spot where the two pilots were hiding.

Strapped to the Colonel's right leg, below the knee, was a holster. It contained a Luger automatic, one of his prized possessions. He had owned it for a very long time, and never flew in action without it. Now he pulled it out and cocked it in readiness to fight for his own life and that of the man beside him.

Three Africans began to move towards his hiding-place, their rifles at the ready. Suddenly, they stopped in their tracks and hurled themselves to the ground as, with a terrific roar, the remainder of the Hunter's 30-mm cannon shells exploded, spewing white-hot shrapnel everywhere. The Africans scrambled to their feet and, yelling in terror, fled back into the trees beyond the wreck. A minute later, the Colonel heard the truck's engine start up again, its note rising as the vehicle moved away. The Kerewatan soldiers had clearly lost all desire to investigate further.

George Yeoman groaned and opened his eyes. Everything in front of him was blurred, and the whole of his body, especially the right side of his face, ached abominably. He struggled to sit up and immediately fell back, gasping, as pain lanced through his spine.

A pale mist slowly coalesced and swam into focus through the blur. It was the face of a man. He stared at it in disbelief as its mouth formed words.

'So, George, you have woken up.'

Yeoman tried to speak, failed, and tried again, this time with success.

'Richter, Joachim Richter. Is it you, or am I dreaming?'

The other nodded. 'It's me, all right. And I have to tell you that I have just had the dubious pleasure of shooting you down. Not that it made much difference, because I flew into debris from your aircraft, and here I am. We are both in the same pickle, as the English say.'

'In the same *boat*,' Yeoman corrected him. The comment was so ludicrous that they both started to laugh. They laughed until the tears ran down their faces and the reaction oozed out of them.

Richter. Formerly a colonel in Hitler's Luftwaffe and the commander of one of its elite fighter units, Jagdgeschwader 66, his wartime career had closely matched Yeoman's own. Both of them had been blooded in action during the Battle of France; both of them had survived five years of almost continuous combat flying. Their paths had crossed in action on more than one occasion, as they discovered when they compared experiences after the war. The last time had been early in May 1945, when Richter, together with his adjutant, Hasso von Gleiwitz, had made his escape from the madhouse of Hitler's bunker and the ruins of Berlin, which was encircled by the Russians; they had got away in a flying-boat, which had taken off from one of Berlin's lakes.

That flying-boat had also brought to safety a key SOE agent and several German scientists who had been working on Germany's atomic bomb project. The name of the agent was Julia Connors, later to become Julia Yeoman. And it was Yeoman's fighter squadron which had escorted the aircraft into Allied territory.

Yeoman and Richter had kept in touch with one another for some time after the war, then their correspondence had gradually petered out. The reason, Yeoman knew now, was not hard to find. The life of a mercenary was not conducive to regular letter-writing.

He looked at Richter, and felt the years roll away. 'I'm bloody annoyed,' he grunted, 'about you shooting me down. It should have been the other way round.'

Richter grinned at him. 'Well, I tried to do it for five years, and never succeeded,' he said. 'Better late than never.' Suddenly, his face grew sober.

'I have not forgotten, George, that I owe my life to you,' he said quietly. 'If I had known it was you up there, I would not have tried quite so hard. I should have guessed it was you, though, by the way you flew. I knew that you were in command of the RAF squadron in Warambe.'

'We need not have fought at all,' Yeoman said. Briefly, for it hurt to speak, he told Richter of the Kerewatan Army's revolt and the British plan to bring out Nkrombe. The mercenary forces, he said, would have to battle their way out of Kerewata.

'Well,' said Richter thoughtfully, 'they ought to be quite capable of doing that. It doesn't leave you and me with much choice, though; our only way out of this mess is eastwards, towards the river. Can you walk?'

'I don't even know if I can stand up,' Yeoman said ruefully. 'My back got a hell of a jolt when I ejected. But here goes.'

Again, more slowly this time, he eased himself into a sitting position, wincing with the pain. Beads of sweat stood out on his forehead, and he looked up helplessly at the German.

'Give me a hand, will you?' he gasped.

Richter obligingly swung Yeoman's arm around his neck and helped the Englishman to stand upright. Yeoman took a faltering step and cried out in agony, causing Richter to lower him to the ground again. 'Christ,' Yeoman groaned, 'this is bloody well impossible!'

Richter sensed that shock and pain were combining to cloud Yeoman's powers of reason. 'Nothing is impossible,' he said firmly. 'We are going to get out of this hole, even if I have to carry you. What we need, first of all, is a plan of action.' He glanced across the forest at the remains of the Hunter, which continued to belch forth large volumes of smoke.

'The smoke is bound to attract somebody,' he pointed out. 'While you were unconscious, a truck-load of Africans came to have a look, but they went away again. There will probably be more. I think the best thing we can do is hole up somewhere near the road and wait for a while to see what happens. If our boys are fighting their way out, as you say, they will come along that rood sooner or later; there is nowhere else to go.'

A distant thud and a spatter of shots suddenly startled the two men. Then Richter grinned and relaxed. 'That must be the ammunition cooking off in my Sabre,' he said. 'It crashed somewhere to the south of here. Nothing to worry about.' He looked down at Yeoman's suffering figure. 'All right, it's time we moved. Sorry if this is going to hurt, but it can't be helped.'

Again, as gently as he could, he pulled Yeoman upright. The pain was worse than anything Yeoman had ever experienced. Blood flowed from his lower lip as he bit into it; then, mercifully, he passed out.

*

Back at the airfield, a savage fire-fight had developed as the mercenaries and a few loyal Africans, joined now by de Salis and his small but highly effective group, beat off the first assault by the rebel Kerewatans. The latter, supported by an armoured car, made a direct assault on the northern perimeter, where the main defences were concentrated.

Koppejans and his men were ready for them. Dug into positions which were well protected by logs and bags of earth, they waited until the armoured car advanced right on to the airfield and then hit it with a single round from a bazooka. A plume of smoke shot from the armoured vehicle's turret and it continued for a few yards on a wavering course, its crew dead inside, before slewing off to one side and coming to a halt. The African troops who had accompanied it, sheltering behind its bulk, were cut down by machine-gun fire.

After that, there was a ten-minute lull during which Koppejans conferred with de Salis. The two commanders retired to the operations room that had been used by the mercenary squadron and pored over a map together. It was apparent to both of them that breaking out of Kerewata would be a difficult business.

'We have to face it,' Koppejans said. 'They've got us pinned down. God knows how many of them there are out there, but they probably outnumber us ten to one. What's more, they've got some artillery.'

As though to emphasize his words, a shell exploded with a crash a hundred yards away, rattling the building.

'Fortunately,' Koppejans continued, 'they are not very accurate, but if they keep it up they are bound to hit something sooner or later. Our boys should be okay as long as they stay in their positions, but the moment they make a move out into the open they will take some casualties. I want to avoid that.'

De Salis scrutinized the map. 'The main road to Warambe lies to the north of the airfield,' he mused, 'and the Kerewatans are between the road and ourselves. The quickest way out is obviously by road and we've enough transport to accommodate everyone, but I don't think we'd stand a chance of breaking through the Kerewatans without some of it being destroyed, and that means we would inevitably lose men. The more I think about it, the more it seems to me that the only way out is to forget about the transport altogether and break out into the jungle from somewhere on the eastern perimeter. Then we can move across country until we strike the road well to the east of here.'

'The Kerewatans will realize what we're up to,' Koppejans objected. 'They have plenty of transport; they will almost certainly move east quickly to cut off our line of retreat.'

De Salis agreed with him. 'That's true. But if they get between us and the river we can nip back into the jungle and outflank them. Our boys are all experienced jungle fighters; the Kerewatans are not. In the jungle, we'll have the advantage.'

Koppejans nodded. 'All right. So we march out. But it's a hell of a long way to the other side of the airfield, and all of it open ground. How are we going to get across there without being cut to pieces?'

'We need to make the Kerewatans fall back from the northern perimeter for a few minutes,' de Salis told him, 'and that very much depends on whether I can summon up some help. The radio equipment in the tower is still working. Give me a little while, and I'll see what I can do.'

De Salis went up the metal steps that led to the tower, a box-like structure resembling the type used by the USAF during the Second World War, and switched on the VHF radio. He tuned in carefully to a particular frequency and began to transmit a coded message. As he did so, more shells burst on the airfield and a fragment shattered one of the tower's windows, the piece of metal embedding itself in the console at which de Salis was sitting. The next instant, the radio went dead.

De Salis' call-sign had been quickly acknowledged, but he had no means of knowing whether the rest of his message had been received. To the north of the tower, from their foxholes, the mercenaries and his own men were firing once more; it was clear that another Kerewatan attack was developing. There was no point in remaining where he was, for the radio was obviously shattered and he knew that it would be useless to try it again. He hurried off to join his men, still carrying his shotgun. It was useless for anything other than close-range work, but it might come down to that before long.

Throwing himself into a foxhole, de Salis wondered how long they could hold out. If the promised help failed to arrive, they would have to try and fight off the Kerewatans until nightfall, when they could try and make their getaway under cover of darkness. But even as these thoughts ran through his mind, a shell exploded on the right of the defensive line, blowing four of Koppejans' men to smithereens. The enemy were beginning to get the range.

The second Kerewatan attack was not much more than a probe, and was easily beaten off. For the next half-hour or so the Kerewatans contented themselves with sporadic shelling of the airfield, but the mercenaries and the Special Force men kept their heads well down and there were no further casualties.

Suddenly, the shelling stopped, and for a few minutes a heavy silence hung over the field. Then the silence was broken by the rumble of heavy engines, accompanied by a metallic clattering. De Salis and Koppejans both recognized it immediately for what it was.

'We're in trouble now,' Koppejans told the Englishman quietly. 'That shell that killed some of my men a while back — it also destroyed the bazooka.'

De Salis said nothing. His eyes were on the fringe of forest that stretched along the airfield's northern perimeter, where the Kerewatan forces were concealed. A minute later, the bulky shapes of two Sherman tanks came lumbering out of the trees.

'Where did they dig those up from?' de Salis asked the Belgian.

Koppejans swore. 'Damn it to hell, I'd forgotten about those. They've been unserviceable for weeks. God knows how they managed to get them going again.'

The tanks came on slowly and then halted just out of bazooka range, their crews not knowing that the mercenaries' sole anti-tank weapon had been destroyed. A moment later, they opened up with their cannon. In a futile gesture, the defenders fired back with machine-guns; the bullets simply bounced off the Shermans' armoured hulls and whined away uselessly.

De Salis assembled four of his men and ordered them to manufacture Molotov cocktails with the aid of any bottles they could find and petrol syphoned from the trucks that stood in the shelter of the airfield buildings. The petrol bombs would be their only chance of knocking out the tanks, if the latter came within throwing distance.

Suddenly, the Shermans began to move again. As de Salis watched, the tanks turned broadside on and churned away in opposite directions, gradually moving round until they were positioned several hundred yards off the defenders' flanks. Once again, the men in the foxholes flattened themselves against the ground as the tanks opened fire, this time with their .5-inch machine-guns.

Clods of earth showered down on de Salis' back. The defenders were now in a dangerous position, for the tanks could keep them pinned down in a crossfire while the enemy carried out a frontal assault.

Cautiously, de Salis poked his head above the lip of his foxhole as the Shermans' fire died away. He spotted movement among the trees on the northern perimeter, and warned the others. The Kerewatans were massing for an attack.

The events of the next few seconds happened with mind-stunning speed. Running from east to west across the northern perimeter of the airfield, at very low level, a Hunter jet fighter streaked in total silence, its wake of sound trailing half a mile behind it. Two elongated shapes dropped from beneath its wings and tumbled end over end into the fringe of the jungle. Instantly, the trees erupted in a billowing cauldron of fire and smoke.

'They're using napalm,' Koppejans shouted above the shriek of the Hunter's engine. 'That'll keep their heads down!'

A second Hunter followed the first, and then a third. Each unloaded its cargo of napalm into the forest. Clouds of blazing petroleum jelly boiled up into the morning air. De Salis shuddered slightly; he had seen what napalm could do to unprotected troops in Korea.

Suddenly, he swung round as a fourth Hunter appeared overhead, circling. It carried rockets under its wings, and he knew at once what the pilot intended to do. He screamed 'Take cover!' and the men disappeared liked magic into their foxholes.

Several hundred feet above them, Flight Lieutenant Neil Hart armed his 2-inch rocket projectiles and curved into a diving turn, hurtling low across the airfield towards the Sherman tank on the right of the defensive positions. The tank leaped towards him in his sight and he pressed the button, feeling a slight jolt as four rockets whooshed away from their underwing rails.

The grey smoke trails of the armour-piercing projectiles converged on the tank. Two of them missed the target and the warheads buried themselves in the ground to explode in twin geysers of soil and smoke; the other two disappeared into the tank where the turret joined the hull. Hart pulled hard on the stick and rocketed up in a climb. Turning and looking back, he was in time to see the Sherman's turret sailing high into the air on top of a plume of black smoke.

He turned and went for the second tank, which was retreating at high speed towards the forest, and attacked it from dead astern. This time, one of his remaining rockets hit the vulnerable engine compartment at the rear of the armoured vehicle. It slewed to a stop, a mass of flames, and seconds later exploded with a thud that shook the airfield.

Under cover of the dark smoke clouds that drifted across the field, the mercenaries and the Special Force men abandoned their foxholes and, in small groups, made their break towards the eastern perimeter. With them, on a litter, they carried Peter Gibbons, who was unable to walk because of his broken ankle and who had been sheltering in one of the airfield buildings. As they ran, a solitary stream of machine-gun fire lanced at them from the inferno of the forest and one of the mercenaries screamed as his legs gave way under him and he fell sprawling headlong on the ground. Koppejans ran back and bent over the man; the spreading red stain at the base of his spine told its own story.

The mercenary was still conscious and in agony. 'Don't let them take me alive,' he sobbed. Without emotion, Koppejans pulled out his revolver and shot him through the back of the head. Then he turned and sprinted after the others towards the sheltering darkness of the jungle.

Chapter Twelve

YEOMAN LAY IN THE SODDEN UNDERGROWTH, HIS INJURED back throbbing. It had rained again and he was soaked to the skin, but he did not really mind that discomfort; at least the rain had helped to alleviate the greater discomfort of thirst. Hunger was not a problem; both he and Richter had carried chocolate in the pockets of their flying overalls, and they had rationed it out between them.

'I wonder what's happening now?' Yeoman said. His companion shrugged, knowing that it was useless to speculate. They had both heard the sound of explosions and gunfire from the direction of the airfield, and had also heard the noise of Avon engines as the Hunters flew overhead. But that had been hours ago, and there was still no sign of any friendly forces approaching from the west along the nearby road. Yeoman was beginning to fear that the worst had happened.

The light was beginning to fade when the two men heard the sound of engines. Through a gap in the undergrowth they could see a section of the road, and a couple of minutes later a truck crawled past, laden with troops. They were Kerewatans. During the next few minutes Yeoman and Richter counted six more trucks; the vehicles moved on past their hiding-place, the sound of their engines fading and then ceasing altogether.

'It sounds as though they've stopped a mile or so up the road,' Yeoman said. 'I wonder what they're up to?'

Richter thought for a moment, then said: 'I think I know. Our boys — or at least some of them — must have managed to break out from the airfield into the jungle. They'll be heading across country towards the road. The Kerewatans must be trying to cut them off.'

'That's exactly what they are trying to do,' a voice said. Richter spun round startled, and saw nothing. Then a shadow moved, and resolved itself into the figure of a man. He wore a green-and-black dappled camouflage suit, and a hood that concealed most of his face.

The stranger came forward and rolled up the hood. A sunburned face grinned down at Yeoman.

'Hello, George,' the face said. 'Looks as though you've got yourself into a bit of a fix.'

Yeoman stared at him in amazement. The coincidence of meeting Richter had been astonishing enough; this was unbelievable.

'Peter. I might have known you'd be mixed up in this business.'

De Salis held up a hand, flashing a sidelong glance at Richter. 'No names, George, if you don't mind. Who's this?' Yeoman told him, and de Salis nodded.

He studied the German for a moment without speaking, then turned towards the jungle and gave a low, bird-like whistle. Instantly, the trees sprouted men, the shadowy figures of the Special Force commandos followed a few moments later by Koppejans' mercenaries, the latter still carrying Peter Gibbons on his litter. Yeoman was delighted to see him, having believed that the young pilot had been killed when his Hunter was shot down.

'The Kerewatans are blocking the road ahead,' Yeoman told de Salis, who nodded again.

'We know. Thought they'd have done it a lot earlier.'

De Salis introduced Koppejans, who shook hands with Yeoman and then greeted Richter enthusiastically. His men, meanwhile, stripped off their packs and made themselves at ease among the trees, well out of sight of anyone who happened to be passing along the road.

Yeoman looked up at de Salis and said, 'You don't seem to be in much of a hurry.'

The Special Force officer grinned. 'We've got a patrol out,' he said. 'They're finding out exactly where the Kerewatans are and what they are doing. They should be back inside an hour. Meanwhile, we wait. Are you badly hurt?' De Salis felt a concern he did not show.

'Jolted my back when I banged out,' Yeoman told him. 'Can't walk. Apart from that, and a few cuts and bruises, I'm as fit as a fiddle.' He smiled ruefully.

De Salis immediately ordered some of his men to improvise a litter, which they did quickly and efficiently. For the first time in his life, Yeoman felt himself to be a useless burden. De Salis sensed it, and tried to take Yeoman's mind off his injuries by telling him about the events of the morning, leading up to the escape into the forest. He had just concluded his tale when three of his men appeared as if from nowhere, breathing hard. They had obviously lost no time in returning to make their report after their reconnaissance of the Kerewatan positions.

The Kerewatans had picked their spot carefully, about a mile to the east where the road was flanked on both sides by a swamp. The swamp was extensive, and on either side of it the jungle was primary in nature and virtually impassable. The road was the only way through, and the Kerewatans had blocked it with a barricade of fallen trees behind which they had mounted heavy machine-guns. Moreover, they were well dug in on the eastern side of the swamp.

The area in front of the road-block was clear of cover for a hundred yards or more; anyone attempting to make a frontal assault on the objective would almost certainly be cut down before they had gone twenty.

'We've got a problem,' Koppejans said, which was something of an understatement.

'Is there no chance at all of crossing the swamp during the night?'

The NCO in charge of the Special Force patrol shook his head emphatically. 'None at all. There might be a way across, but only the local natives will know about it. I wouldn't risk it in daylight, let alone at night.'

'Then somehow we've got to knock out that road block,' de Salis declared. He looked up through the trees at the rapidly vanishing daylight. 'Let's move up and get into position. The enemy will be expecting us to try something during the hours of darkness, so we won't try anything until dawn. Then we'll hit them. I don't quite know how,' he added, under his breath.

Within five minutes the Special Force men and the mercenaries were moving stealthily through the forest parallel with the road, carrying Gibbons and Yeoman along with them. A patrol probed ahead of the main body, clearing the way. Within an hour, the whole force had reached the western fringes of the swamp and the men silently went to ground, preparing for a sleepless and vigilant night. It was still just light enough to see the road block, and they caught an occasional glimpse of a helmeted head as a Kerewatan soldier showed himself carelessly. Then the darkness closed in, blotting out the scene.

It was the most miserable night Yeoman had been forced to endure since the time in that fearsome winter of 1944-45, when he had escaped from German-held territory in Holland after his Tempest fighter had been shot down. Now, adding to the discomfort of the cold and damp that descended on the forest like a blanket, was the pain of his injured spine. More than once, he found himself biting on his already-mangled lower lip to prevent a tell-tale cry bursting from him; in the end, he quietly asked Richter to give him a piece of wood, on which he could bite if the pain became too bad to bear in silence.

He supposed, later, that he must have passed out. When he regained his senses, a thin grey light was filtering through the trees and the forest was echoing to the sound of gunfire. De Salis, bent low, darted across to him.

'What's happening?' Yeoman croaked, his mouth and throat like sandpaper. De Salis looked grim.

'The Kerewatans are behind us, as well as in front,' he said. 'They came up during the night, and God knows why they didn't attack then. They could have been all over us. We don't know how many there are, but they're just sniping at us for the moment. Keep your head down behind that tree and use this, if you have to.' He thrust an M-I carbine into the pilot's hands.

'Where's Richter?' Yeoman wanted to know. De Salis pointed, and Yeoman made out the figure of the German, nestling among some tree roots near the road. As Yeoman watched, Richter's carbine barked twice and there was a high-pitched scream from among the trees somewhere on the other side of the road. Richter's marksmanship was clearly as expert on the ground as it was in the air.

De Salis dragged Yeoman's litter into the shelter of the tree trunk and hurried away. Yeoman found himself next to Peter Gibbons, who was also armed. Gibbons, although in great pain from his smashed ankle, seemed cheerful enough. 'It doesn't look as though you and I are going anywhere for the time being, sir,' he commented. 'Still, this is better than waiting and wondering what's going to happen. Care for a swallow of this?' He handed Yeoman a hip flask. It contained raw whisky, and Yeoman coughed as the fiery spirit coursed down his throat. 'Courtesy of the mercenary commander,' Gibbons smiled.

Yeoman handed back the flask, then frowned as he spotted something in the grey twilight. He nudged Gibbons and pointed.

'See that bush over there, about a hundred yards away over the road?' The other pilot nodded.

'Well,' Yeoman said, 'it wasn't there yesterday. I know, because I remember thinking just before nightfall how open that strip of ground was. I think it might be worth a spot of target practice.'

He and Gibbons injected a round into the breeches of their carbines and took careful aim, laying their sights close to the base of the bush. They fired almost at the same instant, and were disappointed when their shots produced no result. Then, a good five seconds later, the head and shoulders of a man rose above the bush. He stood upright and remained there for a moment, as motionless as a statue, before crumpling sideways to the muddy ground.

'Ah,' Gibbons said. 'Delayed action.' Richter, who had seen what happened, looked at them from his position among the roots and raised a thumb, grinning.

During the next few minutes, the fire from the Kerewatans intensified. A heavy machine-gun, placed behind the cover of some fallen trees, sprayed the area with bullets every few seconds. Its position was quickly located and two Special Force commandoes crept forward inch by inch, their camouflage suits rendering them almost invisible, until they were within yards of the enemy position. Two hand-grenades curved through the air and exploded with a crack, obliterating the machine-gun's crew. The two Special Force men retreated under cover of a withering fire laid down by their colleagues, but one of them was hit twice in the back only yards from safety. Two more men dashed out and dragged him under cover, but there was nothing anyone could do for him. He died a few minutes later.

De Salis came back to speak to Yeoman. 'We're tightening our defensive perimeter,' he told the RAF officer. 'It's as I feared — there are more of them out there than we thought at first, and they're trying to push us back towards the swamp.' His face was grim. 'I don't know how much longer we can hold out,' he said. 'Our ammunition is starting to run low.'

De Salis looked round sharply as the forest echoed to a fresh burst of firing, then said: 'I have to go now. Maybe we aren't going to get away with it this time, George. If not — well, you know what to do, if the worst comes to the worst.' He tapped Yeoman's carbine significantly, and the pilot nodded.

'Good luck, Peter,' he said, and shook the other's hand. There was nothing more to add. De Salis hurried away to join the others, and the two pilots settled down to await what now seemed an inevitable outcome.

'If they rush us,' Yeoman told Gibbons quietly, 'kill as many as you can, but keep one round. You know what I mean.' Gibbons nodded; he was familiar with the tales of atrocity.

A few minutes later, with the battle still raging, Yeoman heard the thunder of a jet engine overhead. Gibbons looked up hopefully. 'One of our Hunters, sir. Maybe they'll try to do something ... ' His voice trailed away as he realized the impossibility of the situation.

'I know what you're thinking,' Yeoman said, 'and there's no chance. Our chaps might have spotted the Kerewatan trucks, if they haven't been placed under cover, but they have no way of knowing where we are and they won't risk an air strike for fear of hitting us. I'm afraid we can't rely on any air support. There's only one way out, and that's through the road block on the other side of the swamp. You may not have noticed, but there's been no firing from that direction so far. They must be saving their ammunition in case we decide to make a break for it.'

The defenders were beginning to take casualties as the Kerewatan fire grew more accurate. Before long, a dozen wounded men had been pulled back to where Yeoman and Gibbons lay. Some of them were still capable of firing their weapons and, like the two pilots, were prepared to sell their lives dearly if their comrades were overwhelmed. Equally, they were determined that their friends who were more seriously injured should not be taken alive by the enemy.

Slowly, the defenders were pushed back until they formed a tight semi-circle around the wounded men. They had a good field of fire from this new position, for the trees in front of them were thinly scattered, with a good deal of open ground between. Some Kerewatan troops who tried to dash forward and take cover behind some of the closer trees were shot down before they had gone ten yards.

Suddenly, there was a lull in the firing. A heavy silence descended on the jungle, broken only by a spatter of metallic clicks as men inserted fresh magazines of ammunition — their last magazines, in most cases — into their weapons.

Then the chanting started. The primeval sound of Africa, it swelled to a crescendo, died away and then grew in volume again, punctuated by a voice that shouted something in a high-pitched scream at regular intervals. Koppejans, crouching beside Yeoman, spat on the ground.

'Somebody's whipping them up into a frenzy,' he muttered. 'A few minutes of that, and they'll have plucked up enough nerve to charge us, regardless of casualties.'

The undulating chant was taken up by the Kerewatans on the other side of the swamp. The trees shuddered to the rhythm of it, and Yeoman felt his flesh creep. 'Now we know how they must have felt at Rorke's Drift,' he said to Gibbons. The latter, who had never heard of Rorke's Drift, or the epic stand made there by the South Wales Borderers against two thousand Zulus, looked at him questioningly and made no comment.

As though a knife had sliced through it, the chanting stopped. 'Let 'em come,' de Salis told his men quietly. 'Let 'em come, and make sure of every shot.'

A fearsome, blood-curdling screech rose suddenly from a hundred throats somewhere among the trees in front of the defenders' positions. An instant later, the trees erupted men, running forward in a dense mass, firing as they came. The defenders hugged the ground and sighted their weapons on the wave of humanity that raced towards them. 'Let them come,' Koppejans shouted, echoing de Salis' words. 'Let them come!' To Yeoman, the enemy charge seemed to unfold in slow motion. The sights of his carbine were on a huge African who seemed to be some sort of officer; he was covering the ground in great leaps and waving on his men, his mouth wide open in a continuous shout.

'Now!' Yeoman dimly heard de Salis' command and squeezed the trigger. The M-I jerked, and the African came on, although Yeoman was certain that he had hit the man. He fired again, and this time the African's head jerked back as though he had run into an invisible fist. He went over backwards and was trampled under the feet of the men who came behind.

The air was filled with the roar of gunfire. The front ranks of the Kerewatans, packed closely together, melted away as the bullets ripped into them. The impetus of the charge died away and the solid phalanx of men became broken up into smaller groups. The defenders were able to select their targets now, concentrating on the groups of attackers who were nearest, cutting them down with deadly accuracy. The rest wavered and then turned and ran, tripping over the bodies that now littered the ground. Blue smoke drifted through the air, stinging the eyes.

'Cease firing!' De Salis roared. The jungle echoed for a few seconds, then was silent except for the cries of the men who lay scattered in front of the defensive positions.

'They'll be back,' de Salis said grimly. He might have added: and this time, we won't be able to hold them. Each man was down to his last few rounds of ammunition.

The chanting began again. Then, cutting across the raucous voice, a new sound intervened, causing the defenders to turn their heads away from the immediate threat and look behind them across the swamp, to where the road emerged from the forest and led towards the Kerewatan road-block.

'Oh, Christ,' someone said. 'Now we're for it.'

Like a prehistoric monster, a tank churned its way out of the trees, its long cannon pointing towards the road-block. The tank was sand-coloured, and Yeoman felt a wild surge of elation as he recognized it for what it was. He looked at de Salis, who was grinning broadly.

'It's all right,' the pilot yelled, breaking the spell. 'It's a Centurion — one of ours!' His words produced a hoarse cheer from the defenders. It was cut off abruptly by the crack of the Centurion's 105-mm cannon. The high-velocity shell hit the road-block squarely in the middle, and part of it disintegrated. The tank fired twice more as it came on, blasting further holes in the obstacle, and a few moments later its bulk pushed what remained of the road-block aside effortlessly.

On the other side of the swamp, the Kerewatans, taken from the rear, were running around like ants, screaming in fear as the tank's machine-gun sprayed them. Then a second Centurion emerged from the forest, adding its fire to that of the first.

The tanks were followed by infantry, dashing forward in short, disciplined spurts behind the cover of the armoured vehicles. The Kerewatans on that side of the swamp, realizing that it was hopeless to resist, began to surrender, squatting down on the ground with their hands held high.

The leading tank reached the western edge of the swamp and halted, its cannon and machine-gun traversing slowly in search of further targets. Behind it, the men of the Cumbrian Regiment advanced more cautiously now, fanning out among the trees on the right of the position held by the mercenaries and de Salis' men. De Salis hailed them and an officer sprinted over, keeping well under cover.

De Salis briefed the newcomer quickly, pointing out the enemy's positions in the forest to the west. The officer was crisp and businesslike.

'Right,' he said. 'We'll push them back and keep them busy while you pull out your men. We have some transport following us. Get aboard as quickly as you can. We have no wish to hang around here any longer than necessary.'

The tanks moved slowly forward again, pushing westwards along the road to cover the flank of the infantry's advance into the forest. The Cumbrians were soon in contact with the enemy, who began to fall back in disorder. Under cover of the diversion, the mercenaries and the Special Force men, carrying their wounded with them, filtered back via the road that led across the swamp, past the shattered road-block and the scattered bodies that lay around it, and embarked on the trucks that were waiting under cover amid the trees by the side of the route. When the convoy was safely on its way the Cumbrians also began to fall back, still covered by the tanks, and embarked in their turn. Within an hour, they were heading back at speed towards the river frontier, spanned now by pontoons erected beside the bridge that had been destroyed earlier. Overhead, covering the withdrawal, the Hunters roved vigilantly, ready to dive down and strafe any pursuers. But the Kerewatans had had enough. They were streaming back towards the provincial capital, their new leaders already squabbling amongst themselves as they quarrelled over their failure to wipe out the white soldiers. It was a loss of face they could hardly afford.

*

'There will be repercussions, of course,' Sampson said. 'Bringing out Nkrombe was one thing; the United Nations had no quarrel with that plan. But fighting a pitched battle in the Congo was quite another. Nevertheless, there was no other way. If we had not sent in the troops and armour, you and the others would not have escaped.'

Yeoman lay in a hospital bed in Warambe, awaiting the arrival of an aircraft that would fly him to Nairobi, where there were better medical facilities. Not until then would he know whether the damage to his back would be permanent. In the meantime, he was doing his best to put the thought out of his mind.

Peter de Salis and his men had departed in the Beverley, together with Swalwell and his SAS. The Cumbrians would remain in Warambe for a while as an insurance against any further threat from across the river, but the indications were that they would have a quiet time.

Koppejans' mercenary force had been disbanded and disarmed, and the men were interned pending repatriation to their respective countries, a prospect that pleased some of them not at all. Richter had been interned with them; he had asked to see Yeoman, to bid the Englishman farewell, but his request had been turned down. Yeoman had no knowledge of this, but he suspected that something of the sort must have happened and regretted it, for he would have liked to see the German again.

Richter's Sabres were still in Warambe, awaiting disposal. The Hunter Squadron was about to depart for the United Kingdom, its job done. Yeoman had received a hint that the pilots planned to invade his hospital room that evening to hold a party. That, at least, was something to look forward to.

He looked at Sampson for a moment, then said: 'It was a balls-up. Not as bad as Muramshir, but a balls-up nevertheless. You know it and I know it. It's time we stopped sacrificing good men in other people's bloody silly wars.'

He could see that Sampson was annoyed by his remarks, and decided to change the subject.

'How is Nkrombe?' he asked.

Sampson looked uncomfortable, and hesitated before replying. Then he said quietly, 'Nkrombe is dead. He hanged himself in his hotel room, only a matter of hours after we brought him out. I suppose that the loss of his family must have been too much for him.' He paused, and stared directly into Yeoman's eyes. 'I'll say it before you do, Yeoman. It was all for nothing.'

Yeoman slumped back on his pillows and felt like crying.

Epilogue

IT WAS GOOD TO BE HOME. YEOMAN WAS ON INDEFINITE sick leave and had returned, with Julia and the children, to their cottage in Wiltshire, not far from Boscombe Down. The proximity of the airfield, and the sight of military aircraft passing overhead every few minutes, had helped to break the monotony for Yeoman as he sat in the garden, soaking up the spring sunshine and taking lengthening strides along the road to full recovery. He was walking with the aid of a stick now, and soon he would be able to dispense with that too.

It was the end of the first week in May 1961 — almost two months since Yeoman had been released from hospital. The long, tedious weeks in bed, while doctors painstakingly repaired his spinal injuries, had cost him a good deal of weight, but now he was beginning to put it back on again with the help of Julia's substantial cooking.

On this May afternoon, he had forsaken the sunshine to watch television with Julia and their surprise guest. Joachim Richter had turned up unexpectedly, looking every inch the successful businessman, and had been staying with them for the past few days. He was on his way to Austria, where he had his fingers in what he described as a 'very promising business enterprise.' Yeoman knew better than to ask questions.

'There he goes,' Richter said, pointing at the TV screen. The cameras followed the rocket as it rose from the launch-pad on a vivid column of flame, slowly at first, then gathering speed as it roared upwards. On the rocket's nose, strapped into his tiny Mercury capsule, Commander Alan B. Shepard was about to make history by becoming the first American in space.

'It's a pity the Russians beat them to it,' Yeoman commented, recalling the day a month earlier when Major Yuri Gagarin had astonished the world by completing an orbit of the earth in his Vostok spacecraft. Richter shook his head.

'I don't think it really matters,' he said. 'Space is something that is open to the whole of mankind — the last great challenge. Maybe that's where our real hope lies, out there.'

They watched the programme avidly, to the point where Shepard was picked up from the Atlantic at the end of his three-hundred-mile sub-orbital space flight — a journey summed up admirably by the astronaut in his own words: 'Boy, what a ride!'

Richter laughed. 'Only an American could have come up with a comment like that,' he said. 'A Russian would have said that it was all for the glory of the motherland, or something of the sort.'

Yeoman smiled at him. 'I wonder what an Englishman would have said — or a German, for that matter? Maybe we'll find out, one day.'

The expression on his face suddenly became serious, and he stared at the TV screen, where Alan Shepard was being greeted enthusiastically by the crew of the aircraft carrier whose helicopters had picked him up.

'You know,' Yeoman said wistfully, 'that must be one hell of an experience. I'm not much older than Shepard. Maybe one day — '

Julia glared at him. 'Forget it,' she said firmly.

Yeoman raised an eyebrow, touched a match to his pipe and made no reply.

Printed in Great Britain
by Amazon